SHIPMENT 1

Wed in Wyoming by Allison Leigh
Do You Take This Maverick? by Marie Ferrarella
A Conard County Baby by Rachel Lee
A Randall Hero by Judy Christenberry
The Texas Wildcatter's Baby by Cathy Gillen Thacker
The Bull Rider's Son by Cathy McDavid

SHIPMENT 2

The Cowboy's Valentine by Donna Alward
Most Eligible Sheriff by Cathy McDavid
The Lawman Lassoes a Family by Rachel Lee
A Weaver Baby by Allison Leigh
The Last Single Maverick by Christine Rimmer
A Montana Cowboy by Rebecca Winters

SHIPMENT 3

Trust a Cowboy by Judy Christenberry
Million-Dollar Maverick by Christine Rimmer
Sarah and the Sheriff by Allison Leigh
The Cowboy's Homecoming by Donna Alward
A Husband in Wyoming by Lynnette Kent
The Comeback Cowboy by Cathy McDavid
The Rancher Who Took Her In by Teresa Southwick

SHIPMENT 4

A Cowboy's Promise by Marin Thomas
The New Cowboy by Rebecca Winters
Aiming for the Cowboy by Mary Leo
Daddy Wore Spurs by Stella Bagwell
Her Cowboy Dilemma by C.J. Carmichael
The Accidental Sheriff by Cathy McDavid

SHIPMENT 5

Bet on a Cowboy by Julie Benson
A Second Chance at Crimson Ranch by Michelle Major
The Wyoming Cowboy by Rebecca Winters
Maverick for Hire by Leanne Banks
The Cowboy's Second Chance by Christyne Butler
Waiting for Baby by Cathy McDavid

SHIPMENT 6

Colorado Cowboy by C.C. Coburn
Her Favorite Cowboy by Mary Leo
A Match Made in Montana by Joanna Sims
Ranger Daddy by Rebecca Winters
The Baby Truth by Stella Bagwell
The Last-Chance Maverick by Christyne Butler

SHIPMENT 7

The Sheriff and the Baby by C.C. Coburn
Claiming the Rancher's Heart by Cindy Kirk
More Than a Cowboy by Cathy McDavid
The Bachelor Ranger by Rebecca Winters
The Cowboy's Return by Susan Crosby
The Cowboy's Lady by Nicole Foster

SHIPMENT 8

Promise from a Cowboy by C.J. Carmichael
A Family, At Last by Susan Crosby
Romancing the Cowboy by Judy Duarte
From City Girl to Rancher's Wife by Ami Weaver
Her Holiday Rancher by Cathy McDavid
An Officer and a Maverick by Teresa Southwick
The Cowboy and the CEO by Christine Wenger

THE BABY TRUTH

USA TODAY BESTSELLING AUTHOR

STELLA BAGWELL

Recycling programs
for this product may
not exist in your area.

HARLEQUIN® WESTERN HEARTS

ISBN-13: 978-1-335-50793-8

The Baby Truth
First published in 2014.
This edition published in 2020.
Copyright © 2014 by Stella Bagwell

This edition published by arrangement with Harlequin Books S.A.

For questions and comments about the quality of this book, please contact us at CustomerService@Harlequin.com.

Harlequin Enterprises ULC
22 Adelaide St. West, 40th Floor
Toronto, Ontario M5H 4E3, Canada
www.Harlequin.com

Printed in U.S.A.

After writing more than eighty books for Harlequin, **Stella Bagwell** still finds it exciting to create new stories and bring her characters to life. She loves all things Western and has been married to her own real cowboy for forty-four years. Living on the south Texas coast, she also enjoys being outdoors and helping her husband care for the horses, cats and dog that call their small ranch home. The couple has one son, who teaches high school mathematics and is also an athletic director. Stella loves hearing from readers. They can contact her at stellabagwell@gmail.com.

To Jason and Karen,
with lots of love.

Chapter 1

"Pregnant! But that can't be!"

Sassy Matthews stared in disbelief at the doctor standing at the side of the examination table. If the roof over her head had suddenly crashed in, she couldn't have been more shocked.

The doctor gave her a kindly smile. "Why not? You're a young, healthy woman."

Sassy's mouth flopped open. "But that happened more than two months ago! And we used protection."

"I'd say two months or a little more is just about right. And no method is foolproof. You did say you're not using oral birth control?"

Birth control! Sassy had never needed it. Then she'd gotten to know Barry and spent one impulsive night with him. Now a baby was coming. It was too much to comprehend.

"No. I'm not. I didn't. But, doctor, I've not missed my period. How—"

"Occasionally that happens in the early months. If you continue to experience them, let your obstetrician know. In the meantime, I want you to take these vitamins until you get back home to New Mexico and see your regular physician." He handed her a small square of paper. "You can purchase them at a nearby pharmacy. I'll send a nurse in to help you dress and she'll give you some information regarding diet and nutrition. Think you can stand now without fainting again?"

With a dazed nod, she said, "Yes. Thank you, doctor. I'll be fine."

As the physician left the curtained cubicle, it took all the strength she could summon to keep from dropping her face in her hands and sobbing. Thank God he'd not asked about the baby's father. Telling him about Barry's death would have broken what little composure she was clinging to.

A few minutes later, her purse stuffed with prenatal care pamphlets, she walked into a large waiting area filled with people, most of whom were sitting on stuffed couches and armchairs. As her gaze swept over the scene, she caught sight of the man who'd been waiting for her.

He was standing near the double-door entrance, his shoulder resting against a wooden pillar. A gray cowboy hat dangled from one hand while a cell phone was jammed to his ear. No doubt explaining to someone that he was delayed at the hospital because of a dizzy redhead.

Oh, my, what must he be thinking? Sassy forced herself to move in his direction. He was the Calhoun family lawyer, and he'd met her nearly two hours ago when the small plane the Cantrells had chartered for her landed at the Carson City, Nevada, airport—and after five minutes of conversation she'd fallen into his arms in a dead faint. He'd rushed her to the nearest hospital and had been waiting for her ever since.

Spotting her approach, Jett Sundell immediately pushed himself away from the pillar. As he strode toward her, Sassy's heart suddenly kicked into a seriously high gear. His tall, lean frame was covered with worn blue jeans and a short denim jacket. A brown-and-white patterned kerchief was tied around his neck, and the square toes of his cowboy boots were scuffed and worn to a buttery brown. She guessed his age to be somewhere in his early thirties; his complexion was a leathery tan while his thick hair appeared to be a shade shy of black. He looked nothing like a lawyer and everything like a cowboy who made his living in the saddle.

At the moment, a smile was tugging at the corners of his chiseled lips, and in spite of the news the doctor had just given her, she found herself smiling back at him.

"I see you've recovered," he said in the same low, graveled tone of voice she remembered from their short conversation at the airport. "I hope the fainting spell was nothing serious."

She was going to have a baby and the father would never be around to be a part of the child's life. That was serious. And, unfortunately, a fact that couldn't be changed.

Trying to keep a positive smile on her face, she shook her head. "Nothing life threatening. I'm fine."

"Good. Then let's get out of this place. I'm not exactly fond of hospital emergency rooms." Taking her by the elbow, he urged her toward the exit doors, and as they moved forward she was acutely aware of the strength of his hand, the nearness of his big frame. At least she'd had the good sense to faint in front of a man with enough muscle to save her from a nasty fall, she thought.

"I parked the truck not far from the entrance," he informed her. "But if you're still feeling shaky, I'll pick you up beneath the portico."

She hadn't asked Jett Sundell to meet her at the airport. But when she'd informed him that she'd be arriving today, he'd insisted on meeting her plane and driving her to the hotel. He'd offered because he represented the Calhoun family, the people she'd come to Nevada to meet. She'd never intended to cause him so much inconvenience.

"No need for that. I can make the walk," she told him. "And I apologize, Mr. Sundell, for putting you through all this."

"Call me Jett. And as for the fainting—forget it. I always wondered what it was like for Roy Rogers or Gene Autry when the damsel in distress fainted in their arms," he said with a grin. "Now I know."

For the past three months her life had been a whirl of grief, shock and confusion. By mere chance, she'd learned she was adopted. Then the man she was beginning to truly care for had been tragically killed. The combined trauma had left her in such a fog she'd not noticed anything going on around her. But now Jett Sundell's presence was penetrating that daze, making it very hard for Sassy to ignore him.

Working on the Chaparral, a huge cattle ranch down in New Mexico that was owned by the Cantrell family, she'd seen plenty of tough, rugged men. But there was something about this man that set him apart and demanded way too much of her attention. Especially when she needed to focus on the news she'd just been handed by the doctor.

Outside the building, the afternoon sun was bright in a cloudless sky. A faint wind was blowing from the west, where a tall ridge of mountains towered over the city. Sassy had worn a light green coat over her dress, and the extra clothing felt good against the brisk January air.

When they reached a black pickup truck with a brand of J Bar S emblazoned on the door, he helped her into the passenger seat. Sassy supposed it was the same vehicle he'd placed her in after she'd fainted, but she couldn't remember their trip to the hospital. One minute she and Jett had been talking in the airport, and the next thing she'd known she was in a curtained cubicle with a nurse standing over her. And now she felt very grateful to this man. Even bonded to him, in some weird way.

Sucking in a deep breath, she watched him settle his tall frame behind the steering wheel. She had to speak up now, she thought, otherwise it was going to make things even worse.

"Mr. Sundell—I mean, Jett—before we go any further, we need to talk."

Instead of jamming the key into the ignition, he squared around in the seat so that he was facing her, and Sassy's attention was immediately captured by his craggy features. The grin on his face was causing a dent in his left cheek and his dark brown eyes were studying her in a way that gave her the impression he was enjoying the moment. Which didn't make sense. No normal man wanted to deal with an emotional female.

"Okay," he said. "Fire away. I have plenty of time if you do."

Feeling a blush sting her cheeks, she glanced away. Before now, talking one-on-one to a man had never been difficult for

Sassy. But what she had to say was so personal, and Jett was such a rugged, masculine man.

"This isn't easy and I don't even know how to say it. But I think I should cancel the meeting with the Calhouns."

As soon as she spoke the words, a look of comical confusion spread over his face. "Cancel! Are you kidding me? After flying all the way out here?"

"I'm sorry," she said feebly. "I realize you've gone to so much trouble—first to meet me at the airport and then this whole hospital thing. I feel awful about wasting your time."

"I've had trouble before, Ms. Matthews. And you're not trouble. At least, not yet. But I do think I deserve an explanation."

Thrusting a hand into her tumbled red hair, she shoved it back from her face while trying to force her breathing to an even pace. "You have to be thinking I must be the silliest woman you've ever encountered. But everything has suddenly changed."

"Sudden is an understatement, Ms. Matthews. Two weeks ago, when we talked on the phone, you were champing at the bit to meet the Calhouns. And hardly more than an hour ago at the airport you were gung-ho to see them. I don't get any of this. I thought seeing the Calhouns, Finn in particular, was important to you."

No doubt about it, she was looking worse than an idiot right now, Sassy thought. "I'm Sassy to you, not Ms. Matthews. And let me assure you that everything about coming here to Nevada was—*is* important to me."

The square corners of his mouth twisted to a skeptical slant. "Why? Because you believe there's a million-to-one chance the Calhouns might somehow be connected to your biological parents?"

She shot him an annoyed look. She'd already explained to this man why she was here. Why was he questioning her again? Especially now that she wanted to leave? "You sound just like a lawyer."

"I am a lawyer," he reminded her.

And she couldn't let herself forget it, Sassy thought. Instead of seeing him as a sexy cowboy with feelings, she needed to remember that he represented the Calhoun family. Everything she told this man would most likely be repeated to them.

"Well, since you feel the need to cross-examine me, I don't mind answering. Although I don't understand the need. We discussed all this before I came out here. Or have you forgotten?"

The sardonic grunt he made brought her gaze back around to him.

Sassy had a spirited nature that matched her red hair. Any other time she wouldn't have hesitated to spit fire back at this man. But learning she was pregnant must have done something to her. Instead of using fighting words, she was fighting back tears.

"I agree it sounds a little far-fetched. At first I didn't give Barry's suggestion a second thought. Just because he thought I looked like a friend of his, this Finn Calhoun from the Silver Horn Ranch— Well, it was amusing. We both laughed about it. Then Barry invited me to join him in Canada for a few days where he was going to be competing in a rodeo. I needed a passport to travel there and—"

"In order to obtain one, you had to have a certified birth certificate," he finished for her. "I recall you explaining all of that. But hadn't you seen your birth certificate before? And didn't you have family who would have said something?"

She let out a pent-up breath. She'd been in such a daze these past few weeks, she couldn't remember exactly what information she'd given to this man. "If my late grandparents knew about the adoption, they never told me. I don't have any other close relatives that might have known the truth. As for the certificate, all my family papers burned years ago when I was seventeen. Before that happened there wasn't any need for me to see the document. Anyway, that same fire killed my parents, took my home, everything. I just happened to be staying with a friend that night. Otherwise, I would've probably perished with them."

"Sorry," he said ruefully. "I'm not trying to be insensitive, Sassy."

This man was rattling her, and it had nothing to do with the questions he was asking. His dark, rugged features and muscled frame seemed to fill up the whole left side of the truck, making it difficult for her to breathe, much less think. And those brown eyes— they were warm enough to melt butter.

"It's a jumbled explanation, really. But I'll try. You see, I applied to the state for a new birth certificate, and when the new document arrived in the mail I was stunned to discover that I'd actually been adopted from an orphanage in Santa Fe. I immediately drove up there and visited the orphanage, but they couldn't tell me anything."

"Couldn't or wouldn't? Adoption files always have a tight lock," he said.

She shook her head. "They don't know where I came from. I was left there mysteriously—in the night. A few days later, I was still reeling from that discovery when I got word of Barry's death. All together, it knocked me for a loop."

The skepticism on his face disappeared as he shook his head. "That's understandable."

Not wanting him to see the despair in her eyes, she glanced out the windshield. She wasn't a loser or a whiner. She'd always kept her back straight and her chin high. And that strong woman was the one she wanted Jett Sundell to see.

"I was still going around like a zombie trying to come to terms with everything when I got a letter from Finn Calhoun saying he'd like to meet me. That's when Frankie Cantrell, my employer on the Chaparral Ranch, suggested that I make the trip out here. In fact, she and her family even treated me to this trip."

He nodded. "Finn told me about his friend Barry sending him a picture of you. He said you looked enough like him to be his sister. And I admit there's a strong resemblance—I recognized you right away. I just hadn't been aware Finn had written to you until a few days ago, when you called the ranch's business office."

Suddenly clearing his throat, he twisted the key in the ignition and the engine sprang to life. "It's getting cool. We need the heater." As he fiddled with the controls on the dashboard, he said, "I apologize again if I sounded like I'm cross-examining you, Sassy. It's just that families like the Calhouns...well, they can sometimes be the objects of—"

"Con artists," she finished flatly. "Gold diggers or nutcases. I appreciate it's your job to shield them from that sort of thing. But Finn did invite me to come for a visit. It's not like I took it upon myself to make this trip. Actually, if Frankie hadn't pushed me, I wouldn't be here at all. And it's not really like I expect anything. But it's been a rough few weeks and this was a chance to get away—to have a bit of a rest from everything else that's going on. And maybe discover some information that could help me find my birth family."

After studying her for a long, thoughtful

moment, he said, "What are you going to do, then? Disappoint her by racing back home?"

"You don't understand. I—" She paused, unable to come out with the real crux of her problem.

"Look," he said impatiently. "If you're getting cold feet about meeting the Calhouns, then don't. They're just normal folks like you and me."

Under any other circumstances, Sassy would have burst out laughing. She'd been raised in a very modest home. And after her adoptive parents died, all she'd been left with had been a small amount of money from their life insurance, a few changes of clothing and an old pickup truck. For the past seven years she'd supported herself by working as a maid for the Cantrells. And though she hardly lived in poverty, she was so far down the totem pole from folks like the Calhouns that it was ridiculous.

"Normal? Jett, their normal would be a far cry from mine. But that's not the reason I'm having second thoughts about meeting the Calhouns." She drew in a deep, bracing breath. "Okay, I'll just go ahead and say it. A few minutes ago the doctor told me that I—I'm pregnant."

A look of confusion washed over his face. "Pregnant? Are you saying you didn't know until just now?"

Just getting the word out gave her a measure of relief. "I've not been feeling exactly like myself lately, but I put it down to stress. The news about the baby was quite a shock. So maybe you can understand why I think I should go home to New Mexico."

"Why?" he insisted. "Is there an immediate problem with your health?"

She pressed fingertips to her forehead and tried to slow the chaotic spin of her thoughts. "No. But surely you can see why my mind isn't exactly on meeting Finn and the other Calhouns right now."

"I can see that you're probably anxious to get home and share the news with your husband."

Even though she had no reason to be embarrassed, a blush moved over her cheeks. He didn't understand. And why should he? During the brief conversations she'd had with this man, she'd never mentioned whether she was single or married. She'd never really clarified her relationship with Barry, either. And now, because she was pregnant, he'd simply assumed she had a husband.

"That would be nice—if I had a husband. But I don't. The baby's father is—was Barry Landers."

His brows shot up. "Barry Landers! I didn't realize you were that close."

The blush on her face grew even hotter. "We were more than friends. And now— The baby changes everything." Bending her head, she closed her burning eyes. "Meeting with the Calhouns doesn't seem that important anymore."

Suddenly she felt his hand settle on her shoulders, and even through the thickness of her coat she could feel its warmth spreading through her, reminding her that she wasn't completely alone.

"Besides your adoptive parents, do you have any other family?" he asked gently.

His words brought her head up and she stared at him through misty eyes.

"As I said, all my grandparents are deceased. There're two distant cousins up in Oregon. I've never met them, though."

He grimaced. "Then the way I see it, you being pregnant makes meeting the Calhouns even more important. If they can help you find your real parents, it would be good for the baby to have roots and a medical history."

Fishing a tissue from her coat pocket, she dabbed her eyes, then lifted her chin. "That's true. But I figure that snow falling in Death Valley would be more likely to happen than me learning I belonged on a branch of the Calhoun family tree. And so do you."

Her reply put a clever arch to his brow. "Did I agree to that assumption?"

What was he doing, she wondered, playing some sort of game with her? With this man it was hard to tell exactly what he was thinking or feeling.

"Not exactly. But—"

He put the truck in reverse and quickly backed out of the parking slot as though everything had just been settled. "Call the hotel and cancel your reservations. You're going home with me."

Dumbfounded, Sassy stared at him. "What are you talking about? I'm not going home with you. I barely know you."

He suddenly chuckled and the sound helped to ease her tense nerves.

"If you're worried about my character I'll stop by the sheriff's department. Rafe, one of the Calhoun brothers, works as a detective in Carson City and the outlying county. He, or any of the other deputies, can vouch that I'm a man of honor."

"I don't need a character reference! I hardly think a prominent family like the Calhouns would employ a sleazeball for their lawyer. I'm thinking of all the bother I'll cause your family by barging into your home."

"That might be so—if I had a family. But I'm a bachelor."

Even though he had that wild and free look about him, the news that he was a single man set her back somewhat. At his age a man usually had a wedding band on his finger and kids at home. Clearly Jett Sundell was not the typical sort.

"Even so, I'm not sure that going to your house is the right thing to do."

"Actually, it's more than a house," he corrected her. "It's a ranch. The J Bar S. And before you jump to conclusions, it's nothing like the Calhouns'. Just a little spread of my own. But it's comfortable. And I think the solitude is just what you need. Besides, if you decide to faint again I want to be around to catch you."

For some reason, his show of concern brought another rush of moisture to her eyes.

She blinked it away and swallowed hard. "I'm not going to faint again," she said flatly.

"How do you know? Your face still looks like a bowl of flour."

"As soon as I get to my hotel room I'll lie down and rest," she argued. "And if I need help, I'll have my phone with me."

"How are you going to use the phone if you're lying on the floor in a dead faint? No," he said emphatically, "it's decided. You're coming with me."

"But—"

"Look, if you're worried about being alone in the house with a man you've just met, forget it. My older sister lives with me."

"Oh."

He looked at her and grinned. "I'll take that as a word of disappointment."

Straightening her shoulders, she settled back in her seat. "It was nothing of the sort. That was a word of confusion. My head is so mixed up right now it feels like it's going to burst."

He pressed on the accelerator and positioned the truck in a faster-moving lane of traffic. "That's what a good lawyer is for. To help a person who's confused and in need."

She glanced at him from the corner of her

eye. There didn't appear to be a tense muscle in his body and somehow that helped to calm her racing mind.

"I don't know if you're a good, bad or otherwise lawyer."

He chuckled again. "Guess you'll have to find that out for yourself."

She wasn't here in Carson City to bandy words with a sexy cowboy parading as a lawyer, or vice versa, she thought. She was here to meet the Calhouns and hopefully find some sort of clue to her past, her parentage and perhaps even her future.

Ignoring his last remark, she stared out the windshield at the passing shops and busy traffic. The desert town was totally different from the New Mexico mountains where she'd lived all of her life.

"Why are you going to all this bother?" she asked after a moment. "I'm not your problem. And you don't have to pretend. It's clear you think I'm chasing rainbows."

"Like I said, you're not a problem—yet. But now that I've met you in person, I get the feeling you're going to stir up a pot of trouble whenever the Calhouns get sight of you."

Turning her head, she stared uneasily at

his rugged profile. "Why would the sight of me cause trouble?"

"Because you are a dead ringer for Finn Calhoun. Only a sight prettier, of course."

Sassy gripped the armrest. Jett's remark was almost exactly what Barry had said to her a few months ago. In fact, her resemblance to his friend Finn was the reason Barry had struck up a conversation with Sassy in the first place. Now Jett Sundell was implying the same thing.

Not wanting to let her hopes run wild, she said after a moment, "It's just a coincidence."

"Probably so. But it's going to be fun to see all their faces when you walk through the door."

Right now Sassy didn't want to walk through any door. She wanted to run as hard and fast as she could. Away from this sexy, provocative man, away from the news of her pregnancy and the fact that her life was taking as many turns as a wild roller coaster.

But Sassy wasn't a coward. She'd never run from a problem; she'd always faced them head-on. And she was going to prove to Jett Sundell and the powerful Calhoun family that she was more than a pitiful orphan without a direction.

Chapter 2

Jett's ranch, the J Bar S, turned out to be more than just a little spread. Ten miles north of town they turned off the main highway and onto a red dirt road, where they passed beneath a rustic entrance made of rough cedar posts. Once the truck rattled over a wide cattle guard, the flat land covered with shrubby chaparral stretched toward the east as far as the eye could see. To the west, low hills were decorated with twisted juniper and ponderosa pine, and behind them, somewhat taller mountains were thickly forested with evergreens.

The direction of the road eventually changed

and took them straight to the mountains, then curved and climbed its way onto a small mesa. Once the truck reached the flattened strip of land, a rambling L-shaped house, nestled in a copse of tall pines and cottonwoods, came into view. Some hundred yards to the right of the house stood several barns and a maze of wooden corrals where a herd of playful horses were stirring the dust.

Jett parked the truck beneath a carport located at the west end of the house. While she waited for him to skirt the vehicle, she took a moment to study his home.

The walls were made of very dark brown logs with natural rock coming halfway up the sides. A walkway made of planked wood ran along the front of the house, until it reached a small porch where a holly bush blazed with bright red berries. Two black-and-white collies suddenly appeared from a far corner of the yard and jumped in excited circles around Jett's legs.

He ordered the dogs to give him space, then opened her door. "Here we are, Sassy," he said, as he extended a hand up to her. "Don't mind the dogs. They love people. I'll help you in, then come back for your bags."

It was on the tip of her tongue to tell him

she no longer felt faint or needed his help to walk, but she quickly bit back the words. The men she'd spent time with, including Barry, had always treated her like a tough, outdoorsy girl who could take care of herself. This was first time in her life that she'd ever had a man treat her like a delicate lady. She might as well enjoy the special treatment for as long as she could.

With his strong hand wrapped around hers, she climbed out of the truck and stood beside him. The dogs immediately rushed to her and she made a point of greeting them before she turned her attention back to Jett.

"Before we go in, I want to thank you, Jett. In spite of some of the things I said to you, I really do appreciate all that you're doing for me."

He smiled at her, and for a moment Sassy forgot everything, including the reason she'd even come to Nevada. There was something in his eyes that made her feel welcome, that said he was glad she was here. But that didn't make sense. Jett didn't know her. Not really. And if he did, what would he think? she wondered. She was a maid and lived on a salary that kept her bills paid and food on her table, but little more.

He linked his arm through hers and started down the long sidewalk. "I have plenty of space and time. And it's not often that I get a client like you."

"Oh. I thought the Calhoun family were your clients. Not me." She would have preferred him to describe her as a friend. But that hardly mattered, she told herself. She was here to search for her parentage, not for a man.

"Technically you're right. But I have a protective nature. Especially when it comes to pretty women. So I'm making you my client, too."

He added another grin to the last of his words, and Sassy figured he'd never had a problem manipulating a woman's heartstrings. But she didn't need to worry about losing her heart to this charming cowboy. She was carrying a baby. That should be more than enough to turn off any man's ardor.

Compared to the Cantrell's elaborate, two-story house back on the Chaparral Ranch, Jett's home was a modest, though very comfortable, size. After passing through a small foyer, they entered a living room furnished with a wood-framed couch done in dark green-and-brown fabric, a matching love seat and two armchairs. In one corner, a television was tuned in to the weather, while a mug of coffee and a newspaper littered a varnished cedar coffee table. Braided rugs added splashes of color here and there across the inlaid wood floor. At the far end of the space, a fire burned low in a rock fireplace and filled the room with delicious warmth.

"Bella! Come here! We have company!"

Jett's shout brought a flurry of movement from somewhere in the rooms beyond, and then a woman with a long, dark ponytail appeared in an open doorway, followed by a black cat with a red collar around its neck.

"Oh! Jett, I wasn't expecting you back home so early." She walked toward her brother, who was still holding on to Sassy's arm, then suddenly she stopped in her tracks and stared incredulously at the both of them. "Who—?"

"Sis, this is Sassy Matthews from New Mexico. She's going to be staying with us for a few days."

Her gaze traveling keenly over Sassy's face, the tall, attractive woman stepped closer and extended her hand. "Hello. I'm Bella Sundell," she introduced herself.

Seeing the same warm light in Bella's eyes

as she had in Jett's, Sassy felt immediate relief. "Nice to meet you, Bella." She shook the woman's hand. "And I apologize for barging in like this. Your brother insisted it would be okay."

"It's no bother." Bella shot her brother a shrewd glance. "In fact, this is quite exciting. Jett never brings guests home. Especially ones who look like you."

"Bella! What kind of remark is that?"

With an impatient roll of her eyes, she asked, "Are you blind? She's the spitting image of Finn Calhoun. A beautiful one, that is." She turned back to Sassy. "Are you a relative of theirs?"

Sassy was amazed by the woman's reaction. "No. I don't think so."

Jett looked at Sassy, and his expression said "I told you so." To Bella, he said, "Actually, Sassy doesn't know who she's related to. And the story is too long to get into right now. Sassy had a nasty faint a bit earlier at the airport and we've spent the past couple of hours at the emergency room. She needs to eat and then rest."

"Oh, my. I hope it was nothing serious."

Deciding there was no point in keeping it

a secret, Sassy replied, "I'm going to have a baby."

Bella's expression immediately changing to one of concern, she reached for Sassy's arm. "That's serious enough. Come along with me and I'll find something for you to eat. Then you can rest." She started leading Sassy out of the room, then tossed over her shoulder, "Jett, put her things in the bedroom next to mine, will you?"

"Sure. And don't go plying Sassy with a bunch of questions," he warned his sister. "She's already had one lawyer digging at her today."

He turned to leave the house and as Bella guided her down a short hallway, Sassy asked curiously, "Are you a lawyer, like your brother?"

"No. I work as a legal assistant, but I took the day off. I had a few personal tasks to deal with in town. And don't worry, I'm not a nosy gossiper. I won't bother you with a bunch of questions."

"That's the least of my worries," Sassy told her. "I just feel awful about barging into your home like this. I had reservations at a hotel in town but your brother insisted I cancel them. Just because I fainted he seems to think I shouldn't be alone. But I'm hardly his responsibility."

"That's Jett. He likes to help people. Anyway, it's just the two of us living here, so you won't be a bother to either of us. In fact, it's great for me to have female company. It's always just Jett or Noah, the ranch hand, roaming around the place."

Since Bella Sundell wore no wedding ring, and was using her maiden name, it was fairly evident that she wasn't married. Sassy gauged her to be somewhere in her thirties, past the age where most women became wives and mothers. Maybe she was wrapped up in an important career, Sassy thought. Or could be that the Sundell siblings just weren't the marrying kind.

A few more steps took them inside a cozy kitchen with a round red Formica table and matching chairs, varnished wood cabinets and a black-and-white checked tile floor. The space smelled faintly of coffee and baked bread, and the scents had Sassy realizing she'd not eaten since early that morning, before she'd boarded the small plane in Ruidoso.

Bella helped her out of her coat, then hung it on a hall tree situated by the door.

"I should've asked if you feel like sitting at

the table to eat," Bella said. "If you'd rather lie down, I'll bring a tray to the bedroom."

Since Sassy's job was to serve others, it felt strange to have this woman offer to do things for her. "Thanks, but I feel like sitting. And don't go to any trouble. A half sandwich of anything will do. Lunch meat, peanut butter, whatever you have."

Bella walked over to the cabinet and pulled out a loaf of bread from a wooden bread box. "That's easy enough. Jett can't live without salami. I'll fix that for you. And to drink we have coffee, soda, tea, milk."

"Coffee would be heavenly," Sassy replied, then her lips parted as it suddenly dawned on her that she was now eating and drinking for a developing baby. She had to think before she put anything into her mouth. "Oh. Maybe I'd better drink something else."

"I have decaffeinated," Bella quickly assured her.

Groaning, Sassy reached up and massaged her aching forehead. "I'm sorry. I must sound crazy to you. But I—well, I just found out this afternoon that I'm pregnant. Before today I didn't have a clue, and I think I'm still in shock."

Forgetting her task, Bella turned on her

heel and quickly returned to Sassy. "Oh, you poor darling!" she exclaimed as she eased down in the chair opposite Sassy's. "You must be in a daze!"

Daze couldn't quite describe it, Sassy thought. But she didn't say that to Jett's sister. Instead, she quickly explained the situation of Finn's letter and her decision to fly out here to meet the Calhoun family.

Shaking her head, Bella reached over and clasped both her hands. "Well, while you're here you mustn't worry about a thing. Jett will help you with the Calhouns. But I'm sure you already knew that before you came out here to Nevada."

Actually, Sassy hadn't known any such thing about Jett Sundell. Over the phone he'd had a nice voice and a patient manner about him. But he'd not seemed overly enthusiastic about her traveling all the way to Nevada to see the Calhouns. So she'd hardly expected this much help from the man. And it made her wonder why he'd had a change of heart. Because she really did resemble Finn Calhoun? Or because, like Bella had said, he simply liked helping people? Either way, she was going to have to be careful around the man and not let him see just how much he stirred her senses.

"Who says she's going to need help with the Calhouns?"

Both women turned their heads in the direction of Jett's voice to see him striding into the room. While he removed his hat and hung it on a hook next to Sassy's coat, Bella returned to her sandwich making.

"Well, why won't she?" his sister asked. "Bart is going to blow a gasket when he sees her. Especially when the family starts asking him who he was squiring twenty-some years ago."

Jett glowered at her. "Damn it, Bella, that's a crass thing to be saying in front of Sassy."

"I'm not a child," Sassy interrupted. "I'm twenty-four, to be exact. And if I do look like this Finn person, as you're both saying I do, then I expect I'll hear all sorts of nasty innuendoes from the Calhoun folks."

Bella shot her brother a sly smile before she opened the refrigerator. "I knew she was a smart girl the moment I laid eyes on her."

He moved over to the sink and washed his hands. "Well, I don't know why you'd think she belongs to Bart. What about his sister up in Reno? Or could be that Orin wasn't always totally faithful to Claudia."

Bella slapped the salami between two pieces of bread, then sliced it diagonally. "That's hard to imagine. Orin thought Claudia hung the moon. He was devastated when she passed away from a blood clot."

Jett dried his hands on a paper towel. "That's true. But Orin has always traveled around the Southwest buying horses and cattle. If he had straying on his mind he had plenty of opportunities."

Heaving out a breath, Sassy said, "Look, before you two say any more about this, I want to make something perfectly clear. I'm not here to cause trouble. And I certainly don't want anything from the Calhoun family. I'm going to visit with Finn—that's all. If the family does happen to have any clues they might be able to give me about my parents, then that would be wonderful. But I'm not here to stir up any trouble."

Jett ambled slowly toward the table and Sassy couldn't help but notice how his presence filled up the room, prompting her gaze to follow his every movement.

"I don't think it's going to be that simple," he said.

Bella placed the sandwich in front of Sassy, then returned to the cabinet and brewed a quick single cup of coffee.

"Neither do I," Bella agreed. She carried the cup over to the table, then went after cream and sugar. "The family is going to be stunned when they get a look at you. And if, by some chance, it turns out that you are related to the family, then you might have a claim on the estate. Isn't that right, Jett?"

Sassy felt sick to her stomach and the nausea had nothing to do with her pregnancy. "Oh, God, this is awful. I would never do something like that. I don't own anything of value now and it's doubtful I ever will. That's not important to me."

Jett pulled out the chair Bella had vacated and eased into it. "Eat your sandwich, Sassy. This isn't anything you need to be worrying about."

"Not worry? I didn't come here to cause family upheaval!"

Because she thought it would help her queasiness, she picked up the sandwich and forced a bite down her tight throat.

He studied her closely. "Surely that concern entered your mind before now."

Sassy shrugged as she spooned sugar into

her coffee. "Sure it did. But not in a materialistic way. My mind doesn't work in those terms. If these Calhouns are more worried about what they own than who they are, then I'm not sure I'd want to be related to them."

Reaching across the table, he covered her hand with his and Sassy didn't know if she wanted to jerk away from his touch or thread her fingers tightly through his and hang on.

"They're not exactly like that, Sassy," he told her. "If they were, I wouldn't be working for them."

Returning to stand at the side of the table, Bella looked at her brother. "Why are you lying to her? Bart probably has the first penny he ever made."

"I don't doubt that," Jett argued. "But family means even more to him."

Sassy looked from brother to sister. She already had these two disagreeing. What would happen once she met the Calhouns? Nothing, she tried to reassure herself. They'd probably laugh the whole resemblance thing away. She'd have a little visit with Finn and then go home to New Mexico and pick up her life where she'd left off. Except that, in seven months or a little less, she'd have a baby, a tiny being to love and nourish. The notion still seemed incredible to her. Yet already she was feeling protective of the life growing inside her.

"So, when do you plan to see the Calhouns?" Bella directed the question at Sassy.

Blinking, Sassy shook away her rambling thoughts and looked at Jett's sister. "After what you two have told me, I'm not sure I want to."

Sinking into a chair on the opposite side of the table, Bella looked regretfully at her brother. "Look what we've done. We've scared her with all this talk about Bart."

Frowning, Jett corrected his sister, "She was scared before we said a word about the Calhouns."

Not appreciating the sound of that, Sassy squared her shoulders. "I'm not scared. I'm disgusted. And who is this Bart?"

"The oldest Calhoun," Jett explained. "The father of Orin and grandfather to Orin's five sons."

"Aren't there any women in the family?" Sassy asked.

Jett answered, "Bart's wife, Gilda, died many years ago. Orin's wife, Claudia, died about five or six years ago. And none of the sons are married. The only women around the place now are the cook and a couple of maids."

"Thank God for the maids. At least there will be someone around that I can relate to," Sassy said wryly, while thinking she might as well find what humor she could in the situation. Crying certainly wasn't going to help.

A groove of amusement creased Jett's cheek. "I told the Calhouns we'd be over tomorrow evening. After everyone has finished with dinner."

"That late?" Her gaze went from Jett to Bella and back again. "Tomorrow is Saturday. Surely you two have plans for the weekend and—"

Before Sassy could go on, Bella interjected, "I'm driving over to Truckee to spend the day with our mother. She's having some friends over for dinner. Jett is staying home and feeding the cows."

Sassy turned a questioning look on Jett. "You're staying here because of me?"

He shook his head. "That was my plan even before I knew you'd be flying in today. I love Mom, but her parties bore me to death. I'll catch up with her later. Besides, I gave my ranch hand the day off tomorrow, so I have to be here to take up the slack."

That meant she'd be spending the day alone with Jett. It wasn't anything remotely close to how she'd planned to spend her first weekend here in Nevada. She'd envisioned herself having a leisurely morning, then viewing some of the local tourist sites. Now she no longer had a hotel or a rental car. Somehow she'd allowed this man to take over and make her entirely dependent on him. This behavior wasn't like her. Not at all. And as soon as tomorrow was over, she was going to do something about getting herself back in control.

Later that evening Jett was in the barn, spreading alfalfa hay for the horses, when his cell phone rang. Checking the display, he shook his head. It wasn't like Finn Calhoun to call this late. Being the manager of the ranch's broodmare and stallion operation, Finn rarely had a spare moment for anything more than work. And at this time of the evening, when the mares were brought in to the barns, inspected and fed, Finn was always there to make sure each and every horse was in its best condition.

Stepping out of the horse stall, Jett used one hand to carefully lock the gate behind him. "Hey, Finn, what's up? Anything wrong at the Silver Horn?"

"Not that I'm aware of. But you know how it is with me, Jett, I'm the last one around here to be told anything." After a slight pause, he went on, "I was actually calling to ask if Sassy Matthews had arrived? You did say she'd be flying in today."

Of the Calhoun bunch, Finn was the one who'd been a close friend of Barry Landers. Several years back, the two men had traveled the rodeo circuit together, with Barry riding saddle broncs and Finn roping steers. And even after Finn had retired from competition, the pair had remained friends. But Jett could tell that Finn's interest in Sassy really had nothing to do with his late friend. It had everything to do with her looking like a Calhoun.

"Sassy did arrive," Jett told him. "She's staying here at the house with me and Bella."

"Still planning to bring her over to the Silver Horn tomorrow evening?"

"That's the time Orin and I agreed on. Why? Are you calling to put the meeting off?"

"Shoot, no! I'm excited to meet her. Now that you've seen her, what do you think? Does she look as much like me as she does in the picture?"

When Jett had first walked up to Sassy in the airport terminal, he'd initially been shocked by her resemblance to Finn. But after a moment, he forgot all about that connection. He'd been taken by the vibrant color of her hair and the creaminess of her pale skin. Her eyes were the color of a cloudless sky and they'd sparkled like sunlight dancing across a pool of water. Her wide, rosy-pink lips had been smiling, and as he'd touched her hand he'd immediately felt her warmth and sincerity. And then she'd fainted and he'd never been so terrified in his life.

Shaking away his wandering thoughts, he said, "I'll wait and let you be the judge of that."

For one brief moment, Jett considered telling Finn about the baby that Sassy was carrying, but he pushed the urge aside. It wasn't his place to reveal such private information. That was her business and hers alone. Even so, ever since she'd told Jett about her pregnancy, he'd not been able to get it out of his mind. She seemed so young and alone, so vulnerable. But then, not all women were as helpless and insecure as his ex-wife had been.

Sassy might be perfectly capable of caring for herself and her baby without a man to support her. At least, he wanted to think so.

Finn laughed. "This is going to be fun. It's said that everybody has a twin somewhere in the world. Maybe Sassy is mine."

Careful to keep his tone casual, Jett asked, "Finn, if it turned out that Sassy was actually related to your family, how do you think they'd react?"

"Hell, that's a peculiar question. I didn't invite her out here because I thought anything like that. She was Barry's friend and she looked like me. I just wanted to meet her and talk about my old buddy. Is she thinking she might be related?"

Jett wasn't sure how to answer that. He realized Sassy was searching for some lead to her biological parents, but she wasn't convinced she'd find it with the Calhouns. "Not really. It's what I'm thinking."

There was a long pause and then Finn said in a mystified voice, "Jett, you sound serious."

"When you see her, you'll understand."

Another long moment of silence passed before Finn spoke. "I don't know how that could be, Jett. Unless she's some distant cousin that I've never heard about."

Or Bart and Orin were hiding something, Jett thought. And even though he'd never known either man to be deceptive, he figured they would do most anything to keep their family tightly knitted together. Even lie. But Jett was going to keep that opinion to himself. Finn had enough problems trying to find his way in the middle of the pack of Calhoun brothers. The last thing Jett wanted to do was have him doubting his father's or grandfather's sincerity.

Moving away from the stall, Jett strode toward a door at the back of the barn. "You're probably right, Finn. It's all coincidence that she looks like you. But everyone ought to get a kick out of seeing you two together."

"I agree," Finn replied with an easy chuckle.

The two men exchanged a few more words before Finn ended the conversation. Jett slipped the phone back into its holder on his belt and, after making sure the barn was securely shut for the night, headed to the house.

Inside, he found Bella in the living room talking on the phone. As soon as she spotted him entering the room, she ended the conversation and rose to her feet. "That was Mom. I reminded her once again that you weren't coming."

Jett grimaced. "I'm sure she's not pleased with me. I haven't been over to see her in a few weeks now."

"Actually, she wasn't upset at all. She's happy that you're going to be spending tomorrow with a woman. I told her about Sassy."

He rolled his eyes. Since her divorce from a real estate mogul up in the Lake Tahoe area had become final two years ago, his sister had been living with him here on the J Bar S. In spite of Bella's doubts that the two of them could cohabitate peacefully under the same roof, Jett had convinced her that being on the ranch would be much nicer than holing up in an apartment in town. And, so far, it had worked. Mainly because brother and sister always spoke frankly to each other.

"I'm sure the news was burning your tongue," Jett said drolly.

Bella gave him a sweet smile. "Well, Sassy is very pretty. And you've never brought a woman to the ranch before."

"Sassy is here because I was concerned she might faint again. No other reason." Except that she had an alluring quality about her that had grabbed him from the very start. Within moments of meeting her, he'd felt himself being drawn into her plight and wanting to make things better for her. It had been years since he'd allowed himself to feel that level of protection for any woman other than Bella or his mother. It was an odd feeling, and he wasn't sure where it was leading.

"Oh. Well, maybe you'd better take a closer look and you'll find a reason to keep her here for a while longer."

Not bothering to reply to his sister's suggestive remark, Jett turned on his heel and started out of the room only to have Bella snatch hold of his arm.

"Where are you going?"

"To change clothes and start supper. It's that time of evening," he said pointedly. "Or hadn't you noticed?"

Bella slipped her arm through his and pulled him over to the couch. "Well, you can give me a minute or two. I want to talk to you before Sassy gets up from her nap."

His expression full of warning, he allowed his sister to pull him across the room. As the two of them sat on connecting cushions, Jett asked, "About what? If you're going to start digging into me about her—"

Bella impatiently shook her head and lowered her voice. "I'm worried about you, that's all."

Jett snorted. "Worried about me? Why?"

She squeezed his hand, and in that moment Jett realized that, in spite of Bella's independent nature, she needed his support. Just as he'd always needed hers. With their mother living miles away in Truckee, and their dad leaving the family years ago, the two siblings had stuck close. Especially after both of their marriages had fallen apart.

"This thing with Sassy," she answered. "I'm afraid the Calhouns are going to blame you for all this."

His brows arched with innocence. "All this? Nothing has happened."

She rolled her eyes. "Not yet. But it will. I'm certain of that, and so are you."

Jett glanced over at the open doorway that connected the living room to the rest of the house. The last thing he wanted was for Sassy to overhear their conversation. She'd probably take the first flight out of Carson City. And he didn't want that to happen. Even though his ex-wife, Erica, had made his life a living hell and caused him to swear off women for the past five years, it was nice to be in Sassy's company. She was fresh and frank, and one of the sexiest women he'd ever seen in his life—which was weird since she looked so much like his friend. And somehow her youthful energy—even despite her faint—made him feel alive and good. He couldn't see anything wrong with that.

"If Sassy's visit to the Silver Horn opens a can of worms, it's not my fault."

"Oh? Then whose fault would it be? You're the man who set up this meeting. Why did you get involved, anyway? If Finn wanted to visit his dead friend's girl, then he should've done it on his own and left you out of it."

He glared at his sister. "Bella! It isn't like you to be so unfeeling. And being the Calhouns' lawyer always makes me the middleman. Anyway, that part doesn't matter. I want you to put yourself in Sassy's shoes for a moment. Wouldn't you welcome any sort of help in finding your parents?"

She grimaced. "We haven't known our father's whereabouts since we were teenagers. And I'm not asking anyone to help me find the man," she pointed out.

"No. But you don't have to wonder who he was. And you have a mother in your life. Sassy has neither. Her adoptive parents were killed in a house fire when she was just seventeen. Now she's having the baby of a man who was tragically killed only two months ago. The woman deserves a little helping hand, don't you think?"

Bella's sigh was rueful. "Okay, I sound awful. I admit it. And I'm sorry. Especially because I like Sassy. I even wish she'd stay with us for a while. But taking her to meet the Calhouns—that's another thing. Let her go alone. Otherwise, if she uses this meeting to start questioning them about relatives, Bart might get angry at you for aiding and abetting her. He might even fire you."

Jett's chuckle held little mirth. "Not likely. Bart trusts me to keep the ranch's business private. But the roof wouldn't fall in if he did fire me. I've been thinking I'd rather hang my shingle out in town, anyway."

Bella stared at him. "I've never heard you talk like this. Are you serious?"

"Very."

Shaking her head with disbelief, she said, "The Calhouns pay you an enormous salary. Why would you want the headache of a public practice?"

"I didn't go through eight years of education to work exclusively for one family. I'd like to think all that learning could help others, too."

Bella laid her hand on his forehead. "My Lord, something has come over you. What is it?"

"I believe it's called maturing." Rising to his feet, he looked down at his sister's worried face. "Now, what do you say about having spaghetti for supper? After the day she's been through, Sassy could probably use a decent meal."

"Are you cooking?"

"I am."

Grinning impishly, she said, "Then it sounds great."

A few minutes later, after changing into clean clothes, Jett left his bedroom and was walking down the hallway when Sassy suddenly stepped through her bedroom door and straight into his path.

Trying to stop his forward motion without bowling her over, he grabbed her by the shoulders and rocked back on his heels. "Whoa, Sassy! I didn't see you coming."

Reaching out to steady herself, her palms landed on his chest. "Jett! Oh, I'm sorry—I wasn't looking."

"No harm done." Easing his grip on her shoulders, his hands slipped to her upper arms. As she looked up at him, he took a moment to survey her lovely face, and the notion suddenly struck him that he couldn't recall the last time he'd enjoyed looking at a woman and touching her, even in the simplest of ways. But he was definitely enjoying it now. "I guess this must be my day to stop you from falling."

"Let's hope tomorrow improves," she said jokingly. "I'll try my best to stay on my feet."

A pale pink color warmed her cheeks, and on closer inspection he noticed that faint freckles were scattered across the bridge of her nose. Her lashes were so long they created crescent-shape shadows beneath her eyes, yet it was her lips that completely stole Jett's attention. They were wide and soft, and he figured that once a man kissed them, he'd want to do it again and again.

Clearing his throat, he forced his gaze to the cascade of fiery curls falling around her head and onto her shoulders. "Oh, I don't know," he told her. "This is starting to get fun."

The color on her face deepened. "I seriously doubt that."

He wanted to ask her what she meant, but kept the question to himself. Just because he found her attractive didn't mean she was feeling any magnetic pull toward him.

And why would you want her to feel anything toward you, Jett? Wasn't Erica enough punishment for you? You don't need a woman messing up your life again and making you crazy.

He needed to heed the voice of warning in his head, he told himself. Just because Sassy was stirring up a hot yearning in him didn't mean he should forget the painful lessons he'd learned in his broken marriage. But, oh, she was tempting him, making him want to believe that a woman couldn't lead him back into hellish misery.

In an attempt to get his mind off the urges in his body, he changed the subject. "Feel like eating? I'm about to start supper."

Faintly surprised, her blue eyes swept over him. "You're going to cook?"

"Sure. I'll even wash my hands before I start."

She suddenly chuckled, and for a brief moment she looked happy. The sight warmed him.

"You're a funny man."

"I'm glad you think so," he said softly. "Because I like hearing you laugh."

Her head bent, causing her next words to be slightly muffled. "Normally, I laugh a lot. But lately—well, things have been a little rocky."

For a moment she didn't stir, and Jett was telling himself that he needed to release his hold on her and be on his way, but having her close to him felt far too good and before he could stop himself, he slid his arms around her shoulders and pulled her close against him.

She didn't resist. Instead, her body settled against his as though it had found a perfect niche. Encouraged by her reaction, he said, "I'd like to change that for you, Sassy."

Her head tilted backward, allowing her gaze to connect with his. "How? You can't change the course of my life."

"You might be surprised about that."

Uncertainty flickered in her eyes. "Jett, I think—"

Her words suddenly halted as his thumb and forefinger wrapped around her chin. "You probably won't understand this, Sassy, but I'm very glad that you're here."

"How can you be?" she asked, her voice little more than a breathy whisper. "You didn't ask for all this trouble."

"I'm beginning to think you're just the kind of trouble I need."

She started to make some sort of reply, but Jett didn't allow her words to escape. Instead, he lowered his head and covered her soft lips with his.

Chapter 3

Jett Sundell was kissing her!

Even though the shocking realization was zipping through Sassy's mind, her body refused to back away and put an end to the contact. Instead, she stood motionless in the circle of his arms and drank in the taste of his lips as they rocked gently over hers.

After what seemed like a long, long minute, his head finally eased back, and by then Sassy was so rattled she didn't know whether to laugh or cry or race back to the safety of her bedroom.

Fighting all three urges, she forced herself to stand her ground and face him. "Is this the kind of treatment you give all your houseguests?" she demanded, once she'd managed to catch her breath.

Expecting him to be somewhat ashamed, she was amazed to see a sly grin spread across his face. "I've never had a houseguest like you."

"So you've not yet learned to mind your manners?"

He chuckled then, and a part of Sassy melted at the warm sound. For the past two months she'd felt dead and frozen inside. This man made her want to believe her life could be simple again. But those days were over. She was going to have a baby, and that would change every aspect of her life.

"I'm sorry, Sassy." He gently released his hold on her. "I don't normally behave like this. But you're just so darned pretty. And—" Shaking his head, he touched a forefinger to her cheek. "It's been a long time since I've felt the urge to kiss a woman."

Sassy found that hard to believe. He'd kissed her like it was something he practiced every day. And with his dark, rugged looks, he'd never have trouble snaring a woman's attention.

Stepping back to put a measure of space

between them, she refused to give in to the impulse to lick her lips. The last thing she wanted was for Jett to think she was still savoring the taste of him. Even though she was.

"Don't you have a girlfriend somewhere waiting for you to kiss her?" She muttered the question.

"No girlfriend. No one special."

All sorts of questions raced through her mind, but she kept them to herself. Jett Sundell's personal life was no concern of hers. The sooner she could get that through her head, the better off she'd be.

"Thank goodness I don't have to feel guilty about that." She started to step around him, but he caught her lightly by the arm to prevent her escape.

"You're a young, beautiful, unattached woman," he said gently. "Why should you feel guilty about kissing me?"

"I'm going to have a baby." As soon as she'd blurted out the words, she recognized how inane that sounded. But she couldn't help it. Hearing that she was pregnant was suddenly making her feel and think differently about herself and life in general. She couldn't be the impulsive, carefree girl she used to be.

From this point on she would always put her baby first.

He groaned with disbelief. "Carrying a baby isn't an affliction. And I do believe that kissing is allowed during pregnancy."

Angry at herself for allowing this man to shake up her senses, she said, "Not by me—or you—or us."

Then, before he could counter that remark, she turned and hurriedly walked away.

Later that evening, as the three of them sat around the supper table, Sassy had to admit to herself that Jett could cook as well as he could kiss. The food was delicious and so was the memory of being in his arms.

He'd called her pretty. Had he really meant that? She'd certainly not expected to hear him say such a thing. He was a man with high standards. She could see that by the way he lived. And, at her best, she had an average appearance. So the compliment could have just been his way of apologizing, she mused. Or, God help her, maybe the fact that she was pregnant and unmarried had given him the idea that she was promiscuous.

Quit thinking about him, Sassy. Forget how his lips felt as they'd moved over yours. For-

*get the way he tasted and the way the male
scent of his body enveloped you like a dreamy
fog. Giving in to a man has already gotten
you into a big fix. You can't allow this one to
lead you down a wrong path. You'll be gone
from here in a few days, and then Jett Sundell will be nothing more than a dim memory.*

She was thankful that, as the meal pro-
gressed, Jett and Bella kept the conversation
flowing with small talk about local happen-
ings and the weather they'd endured so far
this winter. And for a few minutes Sassy was
grateful to have her mind on things besides
the baby, the kiss and the Calhouns.

"Jett, since you cooked, I'll volunteer to
clean the kitchen tonight," Bella said, as the
three of them finished the meal with slices
of chocolate cake.

"I'd be glad to help," Sassy quickly offered.
"In fact, I'd feel better if you'd let me do all
the cleaning."

"Not on your life," Jett replied.

Bella backed her brother up by saying,
"Thanks for the offer, Sassy. Maybe next
time. You've had a long day. You go along
with Jett and relax in the living room. I'll take
care of everything here."

Relax with Jett? How could she manage

that, when just looking at the man whipped her pulse into a mad gallop? Putting her fork aside, she said, "Bella, I'm a maid. I'm used to doing the cleaning."

"You're not a maid here," Jett pointed out.

Sassy had never planned to set foot in this man's home, yet he was treating her as if she was a special guest. Was he just showing basic good manners? Or trying to get on her good side for some reason?

She was still trying to figure out the answers to those questions when he rose from his seat and helped her to her feet. Sassy had little choice but to accompany him to the living room. Once there, she sat on the couch while he went over to fireplace and added two more logs to the low-burning flames.

When he finally put away the poker and started toward an armchair, her coiled nerves had her suddenly blurting, "Please don't feel like you have to sit around and entertain me. I'm sure you have other things you'd like to be doing."

Changing direction, he strode over to the couch and eased onto the cushion next to hers. Sassy's heart immediately kicked into a rapid flutter.

"Trying to get rid of me?" he asked wryly.

Reaching over, he wrapped a hand around hers and Sassy was instantly overcome with conflicting emotions. There was something about Jett that greatly comforted her, yet, at the same time, he made her feel things she had no business feeling. Like wanting and needing and dreaming.

"I should've gone to the hotel as I'd first planned," she said ruefully.

"No. I should've behaved like a gentleman." His fingertips gently stroked the back of her hand. "You didn't ask for that kiss. Now you have the idea that I'm a wolf."

Feeling as though she was about to break apart, Sassy drew in a deep breath and lifted her chin. "There's no need for you to apologize. It was just a kiss, no matter what you think."

Disapproval bent the corners of his mouth. "You hardly come across as easy, Sassy."

She searched his face. "Well, some people back home view me as a party girl—and I have had a few boyfriends," she admitted. "But not in an—intimate way. Barry was— He was the only man I've ever been close to and that happened only once. Now I'm pregnant. Folks back home might not be shocked at the news, but I surely am."

"Every town has its gossipers. You don't pay any attention to that sort of talk, do you?"

"I never did before. But now…"

"You don't want it to hurt your baby," he finished softly.

He understood. For some reason that made everything she was facing seem much less daunting and him seem, oh so special.

"Now that I've learned George and Gloria Matthews weren't my parents, I regard a lot of things differently," she said. "It hurts— the not knowing where I came from. I don't want my child to ever have any doubts about his parents."

"Sassy, I hope you're not thinking that being a single mother is something to be ashamed of."

Her low laugh was tinged with irony. "I'm not ashamed. But it's hard to forget hurtful things that are said about you. For instance, a couple of years ago I had a little crush on a ranch hand who works for the Chaparral. Someone told him I'd like to go on a date with him, and his reply was that he'd never date a young woman who hopped from one man's bed to the next."

"You should have told the guy to go to hell. Did you?"

She shrugged. "After that I knew he wasn't worth the bother. But the whole thing did get me to thinking and wondering why some people get the wrong impression about me." She looked at him, and for the first time in her life, words began to roll past her lips that she'd never spoken to anyone before. "You see, after my parents died, I felt really alone, Jett. I didn't have brothers or sisters. Not even cousins to hang with. And I was desperate for attention and just, well—human connection. I liked going out on dates and having fun. It made me forget that I'd lost everything that was dear to me. After a while, I suppose people began to think I was overdoing it with the dates and the guys. That probably doesn't make much sense to you, but that's the way I see it."

"I'll tell you the way I see it, Sassy. You're beautiful and special. And you're going make your son or daughter proud."

He squeezed her hand, and his touch warmed her just as much as his words. And even though she could hear faint warning bells clanging in the back of her head, urging her to get up and move away from the man, she couldn't budge from his side.

A nervous little laugh slipped out of her.

"I've been talking too much. What in the world did you put in that spaghetti, Jett? Truth serum?"

A faint grin grooved his cheeks. "I didn't put any serum in the spaghetti, but I can truthfully say that kiss I stole earlier this evening… It didn't happen because I thought you were easy. Understand?"

She smiled faintly. "Okay, Jett. I understand."

But, frankly, Sassy didn't understand. Why had that kiss happened? Had it only stemmed from basic male attraction or because he was lonely? Oh, Lord, it didn't matter, she tried to tell herself. After meeting the Calhouns, she'd start making plans to go home.

The next morning, after Bella left to make the forty-five mile trip over to Truckee, California, to visit their mother, Jett invited Sassy to join him on his feeding rounds. After being cooped up in the house since yesterday, she'd jumped at the chance to get outdoors and see part of the J Bar S.

After pulling on a pair of jeans, boots and a warm jacket, she walked down to a big red barn with the two collies, Mary and Max, trotting happily at her side. Once she reached the building, she found double doors swung wide and Jett inside, tossing hay bales into the back of a work truck. Bits of dried grass and dust flew all around him and floated through the shafts of morning sunlight.

Careful to stand out of the way, Sassy watched him finish with the hay, then add several sacks of cattle feed on top of the load. The effortless way he handled the heavy sacks told Sassy he was accustomed to doing much more than just sitting at a desk shuffling legal papers.

When she'd first met him in the airport yesterday, she'd taken note of his headgear. This morning he was wearing the same battered gray hat. Sweat stained the band and the repetitive pressure of his fingers against the crown had caused one of the creases to split and create a hole in the felt.

Sassy had learned to read a lot about a cowboy's character in his hat. And Jett's was definitely full of personality. The fact that he chose not to replace the worn piece of equipment with a new one said he was sentimental about his possessions. Plus, he didn't need fancy to make him feel important. She liked that about him. But then, that was the problem. She liked far too many things about the man.

He motioned for the dogs to jump up onto the truck, and once they were settled on top of the feed sacks, he shut the tailgate and looked over to her. "I'm all set here," he said. "Are you ready?"

She moved to where he stood. "Ready and bundled in my warmest clothing."

"I promise you're not going to be cold. This old truck looks a little rough, but the heater still works great." He reached for her elbow. "Come along and I'll help you climb up."

Once they were settled in the cab, Jett backed the vehicle out of the barn, then steered it onto a dirt track packed hard from constant use. As they headed toward the open range, Sassy wondered if the space in the cab had suddenly shrunk. Jett felt so near she could practically feel the heat of his body and smell the masculine scent emanating from his clothing.

"The cattle are on the other side of this mesa. Not far from here," he said, as he steered the truck in a northerly direction. "They've been getting fed every day so we won't have to hunt them. They'll be waiting for us."

Trying to get her mind off him and onto their surroundings, she peered out the windshield at the rough terrain. "How long have you had this ranch?"

To their left, fir-covered mountains were less than a quarter mile off, while to the immediate right, the land swept away to scrubby desert terrain full of sagebrush and juniper. It was wild and beautiful land with more wide open space to it than the Chaparral, which was surrounded by steep mountains.

"My maternal grandparents, Adah and Melvin Whitfield, used to own this property," he said. "Along with a nice herd of cattle. But age caught up with them, and they decided to scale down to a smaller ranch in southern California where the climate is much easier. Rather than sell this place they gave it to my mother, but she never was interested in country living. She sold the cattle, and I bought her out of the property with the assurance it would always remain in the family. That happened about six years ago, and since then I've been trying to build it back into the ranch it was when my grandparents lived here."

"What about your dad? He's not interested in ranching?"

Jett laughed, but the sound held little

humor. "I learned all I know about cattle and ranching from my grandparents. Dad wouldn't know one end of a cow from the other. And he wouldn't want to learn. More than likely, he's playing rhythm guitar with some hole-in-the-wall band and finding gigs wherever he can."

The stilted tone in his voice should have put her off, but Sassy had never been one to contain her curiosity. Besides, she'd already told him so much about herself, it would hardly hurt him to reveal a few facts about his personal life.

"So, he doesn't live around here?"

The road crested over a hill and took a steep dive straight down into a narrow gully. Jett shifted the truck into a lower gear to slow their descent.

After a moment, he answered, "No one in the family has seen Gary Sundell in several years. He and Mom divorced about fifteen years ago, when I graduated from high school. After that, he left the area."

"And doesn't keep in touch." She murmured her thoughts out loud. "That's odd."

A mocking expression twisted his features. "Not for my dad. He's one of those free spirits who don't believe in ties of any kind. Looking back, I'm surprised Mom and us kids kept him around as long as we did."

"Do you hate him for leaving?"

He shrugged. "Hate him? No. What's the good of having someone hang around out of obligation? I'm a realist, Sassy. I don't need that."

"Hmm. I guess my parents, whoever they were, didn't want to hang around for me, either. But so far I've survived. And so have you."

"Yeah," he replied. "So have I."

At the bottom of the gully, the road curved around a high bank, then climbed to another flat range. When they reached the crest, Sassy spotted a large herd of mixed-breed cows gathered around several wooden feed troughs. Upon seeing the truck, the red and brown animals began to run and buck with excitement.

"They must be very hungry," Sassy observed. "On the Chaparral the winter feeding starts early. We have so much snow in the mountains it buries the grass."

"Winter has put a hold on most of the grasses here, too. My cattle depend on me for a nice meal."

"There the cowboys put molasses licks out

to supplement the alfalfa. Do you do that, too?"

"No. But I've considered it." He cast a curious glance at her. "I thought you were a maid. How do you know about feeding cattle?"

"I've worked on the Chaparral for seven years. On my time off I watch and learn. I love the animals and being outdoors. It's a dream of mine to be able to ranch for myself one day. That probably sounds far-fetched to you. But a person has to have dreams. And I want to raise my child in a country setting— with those basic values."

"You surprise me, Sassy. I would've taken you for a girl who liked the lights of town."

She shrugged. "Visiting town is fun. But a person can't play all the time."

He braked to a stop. "Speaking of town, since Bella is gone I've decided you and I are going out to eat later on."

"Out? But why? As far as I'm concerned, another salami sandwich would be just dandy."

About to open the door, he paused to look at her. "Forget the salami. Even though it's Saturday, I managed to snag reservations at my favorite restaurant. Only because I'm friends with the owner. We might be sitting in the broom closet, but I promise the food will be delicious. Then, after we eat, we'll drive on over to the Silver Horn."

"There's no need for you to go to all this trouble just for my benefit."

As he jerked open the door, he said, "Sassy, you're giving me an excuse to do something I've not done in a long time. So don't spoil it for me."

She hardly knew what he meant by that, but it didn't matter. Spending time with this man was starting to feel very good and there was no harm in enjoying herself before she flew back to New Mexico.

Smiling, she said, "Okay, then, I'm looking forward to it."

Later that evening, Sassy stood in front of the dresser mirror in her bedroom and wondered if she was making a giant mistake. Living on a maid's wages didn't exactly give her the opportunity to buy dressy clothing, but out of the generous gift that Frankie had given her for this trip, she'd purchased a few pieces from a nice boutique in Ruidoso. This evening she'd chosen an emerald-green jersey dress that wrapped across her curves and tied at the waist. The low V neck exposed a hint of cleavage, but a string of crystal beads around her neck would hopefully draw attention away. But she wasn't exactly fashion savvy. For all she knew, the whole outfit was too much and Jett would be too nice to laugh and tell her so.

Full of nervous doubts, she finally entered the living room to find Jett in one of the armchairs. He appeared to be reading some sort of ranching magazine while Walter, the cat with the red collar, sat curled in his lap. The moment he heard her footsteps, he put the paper aside and turned his head in her direction.

"Sassy! Wow!"

She'd had men compliment her before, but something about Jett's positive reaction made her feel acutely self-conscious. Hot color swept over her face and one hand fluttered to her chest.

"Do I…look okay? I mean, am I overdone?" she asked quickly. The blush on her face grew warmer as he set Walter on the floor and rose to his feet. "To be honest, Jett, I'm not accustomed to going to a restaurant where you need to make reservations. And since we'll be seeing the Calhouns afterward…"

"You look beautiful, Sassy. Really lovely."

She sighed with relief. "Well, my employer and her daughter are very classy ladies, so I've tried to learn a few pointers from them. But if anything looks wrong, I'd appreciate it if you'd tell me."

He strode over while his gaze was sweeping her from head to toe. "The only thing I see that's missing is a smile on your face. Put on one of those and you'll be perfect."

She forced the corners of her lips to turn upward. "I'll do my best."

He must have noticed just how nervous and out of place she felt, because he smiled and touched his fingertips to her cheek. Sassy was suddenly consumed with the warmth of his touch, the enticing scent of his body. And suddenly she wished she had the right to slip her arms around his waist, to press her cheek, if only for a moment, to his broad, strong chest.

"I'm going to be very proud to introduce you to the Calhouns. And very proud to share dinner with you."

Was he always this kind with women, she wondered, or was he treating her in a special way?

You'll never be special to this man, Sassy.

You're wholesome and hayseed, while he's a well-to-do lawyer. Just get through this evening without sticking your foot in your mouth or falling flat on your face and you'll be doing good.

"Thank you, Jett." Swallowing the emotions jamming her throat, she turned away from him and murmured, "I'll get my coat and bag."

By the time Sassy and Jett finished their meal and began driving toward the Silver Horn Ranch, the clouds had turned even darker and flakes of snow began to splatter against the windshield.

"Looks like we're in for nasty weather. I hope my meeting with the Calhouns won't be as cold," she spoke her thoughts aloud.

Glancing over at her, he smiled, and Sassy was reminded all over again just how handsome he looked in his white shirt, jacket and creased jeans. He wore the clothes with ease. The same way he smiled at her. As if being with her was as natural as the Nevada snowfall. And as their destination grew closer, Sassy decided that no matter what happened with the Calhoun family, meeting Jett and getting to know him was more than she'd ever expected to get from this trip.

"Are you always such a worrier?" he asked.

Shaking her head briefly, she said, "Actually, I've always been the happy-go-lucky sort. Probably too much so, at times. Losing my adoptive parents made me see just how short life can be. Why ruin what time you have by worrying? That was my motto. But Barry's accident changed me in a lot of ways. Now I appreciate my friends and the people I love so much more."

"Did you love him—Barry?"

His question jerked her head around just in time to see him shaking his head.

"Forget I asked that," he said gruffly. "What you felt for the guy is none of my business."

Confusion, guilt and regret swirled through her, and she stared down at her clenched hands cradled in her lap. "I'm going to have the man's baby. It would've been better if I'd loved him. But—" Lifting her head, she sighed with regret. "To be totally honest, our relationship hadn't gotten that far. We'd only known each other a few weeks and I'd become very fond of him. We were growing closer. But the baby happened because—well, that one night Barry was persuasive and I was feeling…"

"Like a human being—a woman," he finished for her.

A pent-up breath eased out on a sigh. "That's pretty close to what I was trying to say."

What was he thinking of her now? she wondered. That she was the type of woman who didn't take men seriously? Or that she was incapable of having a meaningful relationship with one special man? That idea bothered her far more than it should have. She wanted Jett to think highly of her, to see her as a smart, responsible woman, not as a flighty airhead who took impulsive risks.

"So, now that you've had a little while to think about things, how do you feel about the baby?"

Feeling his glance sliding over her, she forced herself to look his way. "The circumstances could be better," she admitted. "But in spite of that, I'm happy. And I'm going to be the best mother I can possibly be to this child."

"I'm glad you feel that way, Sassy. Real glad."

The sincerity in his voice caressed her like

a soft hand and filled her with warmth. Clearing away the tightness in her voice, she said, "And I'm glad you're going to be with me when I step into the Calhouns' home."

"Don't worry," he assured her. "I'll stick to your side."

She was wondering about the connotation of that remark when they rounded a curve in the narrow road and entered a long lane lined with tall pines and poplar trees. At the end of it, she caught a glimpse of a huge three-story redbrick house nestled against the foothill of a mountain.

This was the Silver Horn ranch house. The Calhoun home. It was even more majestic than she'd imagined, and suddenly the idea that an orphaned maid could be related to this family was completely comical.

Jett parked to one side of the circular drive then took her arm as they walked up a long concrete walkway lined with low-growing evergreens.

At the double-door entry, a young maid, with brown hair slicked tightly back from her face and fastened in a ballerina knot, promptly answered the ring of the doorbell and ushered the two of them down a long foyer.

After giving Sassy a curious look, she took their coats, and said, "You'll find everybody in the family room, Jett."

"Thanks, Tessa," he told the woman. "We'll find our way."

The maid nodded, then disappeared through a nearby doorway. Watching her go, Sassy suddenly clutched his arm. "I'd feel better if I was going with the maid."

With a shake of his head, he urged her forward. "No backing out on this now."

They passed through what seemed like an endless maze of halls and doorways, then finally stepped downward into a long carpeted room with one glass wall that looked over a wide yard and a sky full of falling snow. The space was occupied with several people, all of them men, and it seemed to Sassy that the whole group turned at the same time to stare directly at her.

"Jett! You're finally here!"

The owner of the voice emerged from somewhere in the back of the room, and as he grew closer Sassy was astounded to see a male version of herself walking up to them.

Jett wasted no time in introducing the tall, auburn-haired man. "Sassy, this is Finn Calhoun, the man who wrote you the letter. He's the second youngest of the Calhoun boys."

Dazed, Sassy managed to offer her hand to him. "Hello, Finn. I'm— I don't know what to say. Do I look like you or do you look like me?"

The man, who appeared to be near her own age, threw back his head and laughed, then beamed a grin at Jett. "This is awesome! Just awesome!" Whirling around to the rest of his family, he motioned them closer. "Come on you guys. Come meet Sassy!"

The group of men surged forward, all of them talking in an excited rush. Except for one. The older, silver-haired man was standing a few steps away from the rest of the group, his expression grim as his narrowed eyes burned a hole in her.

As the younger men reached to shake her hand and offer their greetings, Sassy tried to ignore the daunting figure and focus on each name and face. But after a moment, the outsider plowed his way through the men and fixed an angry glare at Jett.

"Get this woman out of here! Now!"

The outburst caused a hush to come over the group, and feeling as though a knife had been rammed into her chest, Sassy turned to Jett and clutched his arm.

Before she could beg him to take her away, Orin walked over to the older man and latched tightly on to his arm. "What the hell are you doing, Dad? You're behaving like a rude bastard!"

Turning into Jett, she muttered close to his ear, "I don't want to stay here. We'd better go."

Overhearing her reaction, Finn quickly protested, "You're not going anywhere, Sassy." He stabbed his grandfather with a burning glare, then turned toward his father and three brothers. "Is she, guys?"

"Not by a long shot," the one named Clancy replied. He stepped forward and reached for her hand. "Come along, Sassy, and have a drink with us. It's really nice to have a woman in the house again. I think I can say that for all my brothers."

"Absolutely!" the brother named Rafe exclaimed. "Bowie, the baby of the bunch, isn't here. He's in the Marines and down in southern California now, but I can safely say he'd be happy to meet you."

Evan, the one with chestnut-colored hair and broad shoulders, rubbed his hands together with gleeful anticipation. "This is a treat. Let's break out the best brandy and have Tessa bring in the cake that Greta made for our special guest!"

Seeing that his order was being totally ignored, Bart Calhoun jerked away from Orin's grasp, then turned on his heel and stalked out of the room. At the same time, Clancy was pulling Sassy deeper into the room and she glanced helplessly up at Jett, who was staying close by her side.

"What am I supposed to do now?" she asked.

He shot her a wry smile. "Maybe you should let the Calhoun family tell you that."

Chapter 4

Wondering if she was being led into a den of wolves, Sassy moved along with the Calhoun men until they reached a furniture grouping placed strategically near the roaring fireplace.

"Sit here, Sassy." Clancy, the tawny-haired one, maneuvered her over to a big armchair covered in cream-colored leather. "It's real comfy and you'll be nice and warm."

"Not there, Clancy!" Rafe quickly protested. "If she sits there none of us can sit next to her."

Clancy shot a droll look at his younger brother. "Precisely. She doesn't need you or Finn cozying up to her."

"Hey, that's not fair," Finn protested. "Sassy's here because of me. I should get to sit next to her."

"Sassy is here tonight because I brought her," Jett suddenly reminded the group. "Maybe the whole bunch of you ought to remember that."

Standing near the fireplace hearth, Orin leveled a pointed look at Jett. "I don't think you'll have to remind Bart of that fact."

From the corner of her eye, Sassy watched one of Jett's brows arch with speculation and though he said nothing in response to Orin's remark, she couldn't help but wonder what he was thinking. From what Jett had told her, he'd worked exclusively as the Calhoun family lawyer ever since he'd passed the bar. If her coming here had jeopardized his position, she'd feel worse than terrible.

Sassy glanced around the group of men until her gaze stopped on Orin. "I honestly think it would be best if I leave." She cast an apologetic look at Orin. "Your father clearly doesn't want me here and I don't want to spoil your evening any more than I already have."

"Forget about Granddad." Finn spoke as he elbowed his way closer to Sassy's side. "He's been acting like an angry old bull lately."

"That's right," Rafe added as he took Sassy's elbow and gently but firmly eased her down into the armchair. "Besides, he doesn't speak for the rest of us Calhouns. If he did, our friends would be few and far between," he said jokingly.

Sassy tossed a questioning glance at Jett, but he merely smiled as though to say they might as well stay and make the most of the situation. It wasn't exactly the encouraging sign she needed from him, but she had to remember that these men were his friends. He probably wasn't feeling any of the angst that was gripping her.

Drawing in a deep, bracing breath, she forced herself to settle back in the chair, and for the next few minutes, the brothers were intent on making her comfortable by supplying her with a footstool, a huge hunk of German chocolate cake and a cup of decaffeinated coffee, delivered especially for her from the kitchen.

Eventually everyone took a seat, and knowing the personal questions were about to start, she was greatly relieved when Jett drew a chair close to hers.

"Finn tells us that you were Barry Landers' girlfriend," Orin stated. "I didn't know the lad personally, but I was sorry to hear about his death. Finn said it was a freak incident. That a horse tossed him into a fencepost and he hit his head."

Strange, Sassy thought. For a long time, Barry's death had monopolized her thoughts. But since she'd arrived in Carson City, Barry's accident was steadily being pushed behind her. Now she was seeing the future without imagining him in it. The realization told her she was healing and moving forward, which was a good thing. Looking backward with regret never helped anyone. Now she had a child to plan for, and that was definitely lifting her spirits.

"By the time I heard the news of his death, he was already buried," she explained. "It was a shock."

No one close to Barry had even known to contact her about his death. But it hadn't been as though everyone on the rodeo circuit he traveled had been aware he had a girlfriend. And from what he'd told her, the only relative he stayed in contact with was his father, who lived in Colorado.

Across the way, Finn cleared his throat. "Well, I just want you to know that Barry was a great friend, Sassy. The best."

She smiled at the man with the auburn hair, blue eyes and features that eerily resembled hers. "Thank you for saying that."

An awkward moment of silence passed, and as it did she could feel Jett's arm slipping across the back of her chair as though to remind her that he was close and ready to protect her. She was more than grateful for his support.

"Well, I'll say one thing," Rafe, the darker-haired one of the brothers spoke as his gaze slipped back and forth between Finn and Sassy. "If Finn and Sassy were the same age, I'd say they were identical twins."

"Identical twins are the same sex," Evan corrected Rafe.

From the short rundown Jett had given her of the Calhoun brothers, she remembered that Evan was a lawman, which probably explained why he was reciting facts.

Rafe frowned at him. "I know that, Detective Calhoun. So can you tell me another reason this woman is the spitting image of our little brother?"

"No. But she also looks like a grown-up version of Darci," Evan said.

"Who's Darci?"

Sassy's innocent question caused Orin to

suddenly clear his throat and Finn to shift uncomfortably in his seat.

"She was our sister," Rafe awkwardly explained. "But she was born with a heart defect. She died when she was only two."

Sensing that Darci Calhoun's death was not something they often discussed, Sassy simply said, "Oh. I'm sorry I asked."

"Don't be sorry," Evan told her. "It's nice for me to imagine her here, looking as you do now." He turned to his father. "So what do you think, Dad? Is there any chance Sassy might be related?"

Orin gave his chin a thoughtful stroke. "Ever since Finn showed us Sassy's picture and Jett explained about her being adopted, I've been trying to think of what branch of the family tree she might have descended from, but I can't come up with anything." The older man turned a pensive gaze on Sassy. "I had an older brother, Dave. But he was killed in the Vietnam War long before you were born. He was never married, and as far as I know he didn't have any children."

"Well, my guess is Aunt Arlene," Clancy declared. "She's not too old to have a daughter Sassy's age. And when she was younger, she looked a whole lot like Finn and Sassy."

Beside her, Jett said, "Someone told me Arlene could never have children."

"That's not exactly right," Orin corrected him. "In the early years of her marriage, my sister had a baby boy, but it only survived for a few days. After that, she couldn't bring herself to try for another child."

"Aunt Arlene always was a little different." Rafe tossed out his opinion. "After that creep of a husband left her for a younger woman, she had a breakdown. She hasn't been the same since."

Orin shot his middle son a pained look. "That ordeal has nothing to do with her decision not to have children."

Rafe rose from his seat on the couch and carried his empty dessert plate over to a nearby table. "I'm not so sure about that," he said. "That kind of trauma can damage a person in plenty of ways. Anyway, she never wanted to stay close with any of us. She could be keeping all kinds of secrets from her family."

"Not that deep of a secret," Orin said flatly, then turned his attention back to Sassy. "Jett explained to us that the orphanage you were adopted from can't give you any information about your biological parents. Do you have any other information to go on?"

Sassy glanced at the faces that were all looking directly at her, then around the richly furnished room. Signs of family were everywhere. From the photos on the wall and perched upon the fireplace mantel, to a shelf full of trophies collected from years of school events. No one in this group of guys had to guess or wonder where they came from or who their parents might be. How would that feel, she wondered, to have such solid ground beneath her feet, to have the support of a family always surrounding her and her baby?

"Not any more than the obvious, Mr. Calhoun. Twenty-four years ago in the middle of the night, I was left on the doorstep of an orphanage in Santa Fe, New Mexico. There was no identification with me. Nothing to hint at where I'd come from."

Lowering his wineglass, the deputy studied her thoughtfully. "Could the orphanage determine how old you were?"

"I'd just been born."

"Aww, hell."

The soft exclamation came from Finn, and she favored him with a faint smile. Along with features that resembled hers, he appeared to have a tender heart. Obviously, he'd not taken after his grandfather, Sassy thought dourly. The damned old man. Instead of letting his outburst hurt her feelings, she should be angry.

"So you were eventually adopted after that," Clancy said. "Did your adoptive parents know anything about the circumstances of your birth?"

The question had Sassy reflecting on her parents, the two people who'd chosen to love and raise her as their own. She'd trusted them implicitly, but now she was faced with the fact that they hadn't been exactly what they'd seemed. The revelation had left her feeling betrayed, confused and wondering who she was.

The touch of Jett's hand on her arm brought her out of her thoughts and encouraged her to share her past with these men. No matter how wretched it sounded.

"A couple from Ruidoso, New Mexico, adopted me. They both died in a house fire when I seventeen, and up until a few weeks ago, I'd always believed I was their biological daughter. Then I applied for a birth certificate to replace the one that had been destroyed in the fire, and that's when all of this about the adoption came to light."

Frowning thoughtfully, Rafe walked over to the fireplace and turned his back to the flames. "Maybe we've been looking at things all wrong," he said to no one in particular. "Could it be that Sassy might be related to Mom in some way?"

"That would be a logical deduction, brother," Evan said. "But you're forgetting that Sassy looks like a Calhoun. She wouldn't have inherited that from Mom."

Rafe let out a good-natured groan. "It's pretty evident why you're the detective and I'm the ranch foreman."

Orin turned a smile on Sassy. "One thing is very clear, Sassy, we're glad you came and we hope you enjoy your stay in Carson City."

"Thank you, Mr. Calhoun," Sassy replied, while thinking she'd traveled all this way to Nevada hoping she'd learn something about her real parents. Instead, she'd learned she was going to *be* a parent. Her life had taken a wild U-turn since she'd left the Chaparral and she had the odd feeling that the ride wasn't over yet.

During the next hour, the subject of her being related was dropped and the conversation moved on to lighter things. The men entertained her with stories relating to the ranch and even included some of Evan's experiences as a deputy. It didn't take Sassy long to figure out that each of the Calhoun men had his own personality, and it was very easy to like them all. Especially since each man seemed genuinely glad to have her company.

Eventually, it was Jett who put an end to the evening, by rising to his feet and announcing that it was getting late and the two of them needed to be leaving.

After exchanging goodbyes with the Calhouns and assuring them they could find their way to the door, they were walking through the huge house when Jett said, "I hope you're not annoyed with me for ending the visit. But you've had a long day. I don't want you to overdo it and faint again."

"I'm not about to faint," she assured him. "But I am getting a bit tired."

"I expect you're disappointed, too."

She glanced up at him. "You mean because they couldn't tell me anything about my parents?"

He nodded. "I understand you considered it a long shot, but you must have held out a tiny glimmer of hope that they might have some good clues as to where you might start looking."

She shrugged. "A glimmer, nothing more. You said you were a realist, Jett. Well, so am I. And the fact is, I might never find my biological parents."

"I wouldn't give up on the notion."

She squared her shoulders. "I don't give up on anything."

"That's good to know. Because after this evening… I'm not so sure we can cross the Calhouns off your family list."

By now they had reached the entrance to the foyer. As Jett opened a small closet to retrieve their coats, Sassy asked curiously, "What do you mean?"

Easing out of the closet with the coats tossed over his arm, he opened his mouth to answer, but was suddenly distracted by an older woman hurrying toward them. As she grew nearer, she placed a shushing finger against her lips and motioned for them to follow her.

Jett helped Sassy into her coat, then shouldered on his own jacket before they joined the woman in the secluded entrance to the house.

"Greta, what are you doing?" he asked

comically. "Playing spy tonight for the old man or something?"

The heavyset woman appeared to be somewhere in her fifties. Short, mouse-brown hair flopped in disarray around a face that bore wrinkles at the corners of her gray eyes and thin lips. At the moment, her plain features were creased into an impatient frown directed at Jett.

"Jett, you know me better. I'd never do any snitching for the old codger. The only reason I stay around here is for the boys."

Sassy supposed "the boys" meant the Calhoun brothers and the old codger had to be Bart.

Greta turned her attention to Sassy. "I'm the Calhouns' cook," she introduced herself. "I've worked on the Silver Horn for more than thirty years and I don't miss much that goes on around here."

"I'm Sassy. It's nice to meet you, Greta." Sassy politely greeted the other woman.

Jett quickly put in, "Any other time, we'd come to the kitchen and gab a few minutes, Greta, but Sassy has had a long day and I want to get her home before the snow gets any deeper on the roads."

The cook shook her head in a frustrating way. "All right, all right. I'll get to the point."

"And?" Jett prompted.

Greta glanced over her shoulder toward the open doorway leading into the house, giving the impression she wanted to make sure no one overheard her. "Jett, you're wasting your time talking to the boys or Orin about things. You need to question the old man about Sassy. If anyone knows about an extra Calhoun baby being born, it'd be Bart. Why else do you think he had such a fit when he laid eyes on her?"

Jett and Sassy exchanged questioning glances.

"How did you know Bart had a fit?" Jett asked the cook.

Greta rolled her eyes. "He was in such a state, he called for Tessa to fetch a glass of milk and a sedative up to his room. When she got back to the kitchen, she said the old man looked like he was ready to blow a gasket."

"Okay, Greta. Thanks for the information. I'll keep it in mind," he told the cook, then quickly hustled Sassy toward the door.

Greta gasped. "But Jett, you need to—"

"Later, Greta. We gotta go."

Outside, the snow was still falling and

drifts were piling against the evergreens that lined the sidewalk. The cold night air felt refreshing to Sassy's hot cheeks, and she breathed deeply as she tried to assimilate all that had happened in the past couple of hours.

"That was a hell of a send-off," Jett said as he helped her into the cab of the truck. "I'm sorry the cook had to bring all of that up about Bart. She means well, but you didn't need to hear it."

He shut the door, then quickly skirted the truck and climbed behind the wheel. As he started the engine, Sassy asked, "You didn't believe what she was saying?"

"Maybe. Did you?"

Sassy shook her head. "Oh, I believe she was right about Bart Calhoun being upset. Dear Lord, you saw the way he reacted when we arrived. But I don't put much stock in her idea about Bart having information concerning me. She's house help and they like to gossip among themselves. I ought to know, I'm a maid at the Chaparral and I'm ashamed to admit that I've done it myself at times."

Jett was silent as he put the truck into motion, but once he'd steered it away from the house, he said, "Frankly, all evening I've been wondering why Bart reacted to you the way he did. That's why I'm not quite certain we should totally rule out the possibility that you might be a Calhoun. The old man can be stodgy at times, but I've never seen him behave in such a rude manner. Especially toward a woman. The man normally adores females. The whole thing makes me suspicious."

Sassy shook her head. "I don't see anything suspicious about it. Evan said that I looked like Darci, their late sister. It didn't seem to bother Orin or the brothers that I resembled her. But it could have bothered Bart. Could be that I reminded him of the painful memory of losing his granddaughter. Does that make sense? I hope so. Otherwise, I don't know why he would hate a complete stranger."

"I wouldn't use the word 'hate,' Sassy. But he clearly didn't want you around for some reason. You could be right about Darci, though. Could be you were like a living ghost to him."

"Have you ever seen pictures of her?" Sassy asked curiously. "I wonder if she did resemble me that much."

"I've not see any pictures. Once I asked why there weren't any photos of her in the house. Clancy explained that his mother had stored away everything connected to the girl. Supposedly, the memories were too painful for her to deal with. Now that Claudia is gone, you'd think they'd bring out a picture or two, just to acknowledge her brief time with the family, but I've not seen any."

"How sad." The notion had Sassy suddenly thinking of her own baby. No matter the circumstances, the unborn child had already latched on to her heart. Losing her son or daughter, now or in the future, would tear her to pieces. "Well, I won't be guilty of stirring up memories for the Calhouns a second time." She glanced over at him. "Earlier you asked me if I was disappointed. Well, to be honest, Jett, I feel badly about coming here. It's clearly caused problems with Bart, and I'm worried it's all going to spill over on to you."

He shook his head. "Forget about me. I'm not worried."

"But that remark Orin made—Bart might want to fire you!"

"Look, Sassy, Bart Calhoun can't make or break me. So put the whole thing out of your head. What I'm more concerned about now is what the old man might possibly know about your birth."

She shook her head. "Do you honestly

think that Bart might know something about my parents?"

"The old man has always been truthful with me. But people can lie when it suits their purpose. And that purpose could be to keep the past hidden in the past."

"If he would stoop to lying to keep me out of the family, then it would be pretty clear I'm not wanted. I don't think I'd want to learn I was related to him, Jett." Her eyes stinging with inexplicable tears, she turned her watery gaze to the passenger window and the snowy night beyond the thick glass. "I'll be going home as soon as I can get a flight back to New Mexico, so hopefully that will put an end to everything."

"Is that what you want to do?" he asked with annoyance. "Hurry back home? What's that going to fix?"

Everything, she thought. She could go back to her old life, her old job at the Chaparral. She could forget all about the Calhouns. And she could especially forget about Jett and how just looking at the man made her heart flutter. But once she got back in her familiar daily routine, would she be able to put Jett out of her mind? She had the baby to focus on now. Its impending arrival would surely be enough to wipe memories of the man from her mind. She had to believe that.

"I don't need to fix anything," she murmured. "I just need to get on with my life."

A stretch of silence passed and then Jett said, "Have you stopped to think that that might be what you're doing right here? Right now?"

Sassy couldn't answer his questions, but later that night in her bedroom, when she picked up the phone to call Frankie, she was still thinking about them. Since she'd arrived in Carson City, her life felt as though it was changing by the hour. It was a dizzying spin, making it impossible for her to know where she belonged.

Frankie answered on the third ring and Sassy was thankful when the woman's familiar voice quickly jerked her wandering thoughts back to solid ground.

"Sassy, I'm so glad you finally called. I was beginning to worry about you."

The woman would've been even more worried if she'd known Sassy had spent her first hour in Carson City lying on a hospital gurney in the emergency room. But, for now, Sassy had no intention of revealing any of that to Frankie. There would be plenty of time for that later, after she'd had a chance to collect her thoughts and map a plan for herself and the baby.

Sassy took a seat on the edge of the queen-size bed. "Didn't you get my text message telling you that my flight had arrived safely?"

"Yes. I was glad you let me know. But we've all been wondering if you've met the Calhouns yet."

"Actually, that's the reason I'm calling. To let you know we went to the Silver Horn this evening. In fact, we just returned a few minutes ago."

"We? Someone went with you?"

"Jett Sundell. Remember? He's the Calhoun family lawyer."

"Hmm—yes. I do remember now. But isn't that taking things a bit far, to have their lawyer accompany you? Are these people paranoid or something?"

It would be impossible for Sassy to explain how Jett had somehow emerged as her protector. Because, frankly, his support didn't make sense. His first alliance and concerns should be the Calhouns. And, truth be told, if he was forced to choose between her or them, it would be the Calhouns. But none of that should really matter now. As far as she was concerned, there was no branch on the Calhoun family tree with her name on it.

"I suppose it is odd in a way. It's sure not the way you Cantrells handle things. And the old patriarch of the family was far from welcoming. But Jett has been very helpful. In fact, I've been staying on his ranch."

"Oh. I see. I think."

The motherly caution in Frankie's voice had Sassy quickly adding, "His sister lives here, also. She's very nice."

Frankie's sigh of relief was evident. "If these people are being helpful, then I'm glad. So tell me about the Calhouns. Think there's a chance you might be connected to them in some way?"

"Not really, Frankie. They can't think of any relatives I might link with."

"Awww! And for some reason I was so hopeful about it all," Frankie said, her voice full of disappointment. "But I'm proud that you made the trip and that you're seeing new things and meeting new people. It couldn't have been easy talking to strangers about such a personal matter, but even that was probably a good learning experience for you."

The memory of Bart Calhoun staring a dark hole through her was something Sassy would never forget. And she'd definitely learned from the experience. She'd learned that having Jett by her side had given her the courage and patience to stand her ground. If not for him, she would probably have turned on her heel and left the house. Mostly out of anger.

"It wasn't easy, Frankie." And prying any sort of information from Bart Calhoun would be even more difficult, she thought grimly. Getting him to spill a secret would be like breaking a piece of granite with her bare hand. "But for the most part, the brothers, minus the one who's a Marine in California, and their father, Orin, were very warm and likable."

"But they had no clues about your family? Did you explain about the orphanage and how you were dropped there?"

Sassy held back a sigh. "I told them everything. They all seemed clueless. So I figure I'm wasting time here, Frankie. I'll probably be coming home in a day or two."

There was a long pause and then a groan. "Sassy, there's no need for you to hurry back. You're just a short distance from Reno and Lake Tahoe. Lewis took me there on one of our wedding anniversaries. I promise, it's beautiful."

Before this flight to Nevada, Sassy had never had the opportunity to take driving trips, much less board an airplane. A few times she'd gone to Alamogordo with friends, and once she'd gone to the fair at Albuquerque. Then, a few weeks ago, she'd gone up to Santa Fe to visit the orphanage where she'd lived as a newborn. But that was the extent of her travels. Under normal circumstances, a chance to see and do things she'd never experienced before would have had her jumping for joy. But right now, the opportunity didn't appeal to her. Not when her mind was being consumed by the baby and all the changes she was going to need to make in the coming months. And then there was Jett. She had to admit the man was doing something to her. Not only did her mind go haywire whenever he was near her, but her body followed right after it. No, she thought, common sense warned her that the sooner she put two states between them, the safer her heart would be.

"The Chaparral is beautiful, too, Frankie."

"That's a lovely thing to say, Sassy. Especially when I know that you mean it. But you've only been gone two days. That's not long enough to get homesick," Frankie teased. Then, after a long pause, her tone turned serious. "Now that I think about it, you do sound a little melancholy. Are you sure you're feeling okay?"

Other than being pregnant, confused and glum, she was the picture of health, she could have told Frankie. Instead, she said in the cheeriest voice she could summon, "I'm fine, Frankie. Really. Now tell me what's been going on there. Did Alexa and her family arrive?"

Frankie let out a happy, but weary, groan. "Yes, and we've been staying very busy. The kids never run down, you know. And Leyla cooked a huge special meal today. Abe and Reena joined us. In fact, they're still here enjoying a last round of pie before they head back to Apache Wells. But Alexa and Jonas and the kids plan to stay through the weekend."

Sassy knew how much Frankie enjoyed spending time with her daughter, Alexa. Throughout the years she'd worked for the family, Sassy had witnessed the unique bond that existed between the two women. It was something she'd never be able to experience herself, and now that Sassy was pregnant and soon to be a mother, the fact hit her even harder. There would be no grandparents around to enjoy her son or daughter.

"I'm glad she and her family are getting to stay a few days. I should be there to help with all the extra household chores. Leyla has Dillon and her new daughter to care for. She can't be cleaning house and doing the laundry for everyone."

"Sassy," Frankie gently scolded. "I wouldn't allow Leyla to even try. We're not helpless around here, you know. Now forget the Chaparral and everybody back here. The dust might get thick and the laundry piled high, but that's okay. We'll deal with it."

With Frankie being so understanding, Sassy was very tempted to go ahead and spill the news about her pregnancy. But she instantly nixed the impulse. With Alexa there, Frankie needed to enjoy this special time with her family. Not be worrying over her maid.

"Okay, Frankie. I'll think about traveling up to Tahoe before I head back," Sassy told her, then went on to promise that whatever she decided to do, she'd keep Frankie informed.

After giving the woman a final goodbye, Sassy placed the cell phone on the nightstand, then lay back on the bed and rested a hand on her lower belly.

She'd come to Nevada searching for family. But it was time she accepted the fact that the only real family she had was resting in her womb. In the months ahead, it would be just her and the baby. And that would have to be enough.

Chapter 5

While Sassy remained cloistered in her bedroom, Jett stared absently into the flames that were licking around the small logs he'd stacked in the fireplace. During the past ten minutes, he'd been listening for Sassy's footsteps, hoping she might rejoin him before the evening ended. But he was beginning to doubt he would see her again tonight.

Clearly, the meeting with the Calhouns had drained her. And, to be honest, it hadn't exactly made Jett a happy man. For as long as he lived, he'd never forget Sassy's face when Bart had ordered her out of the house. Her blue eyes had darkened with pain, yet her chin had lifted with pride, and at that moment he'd wanted to draw her into the safety of his arms, to assure her that she was worth more than a dozen Bart Calhouns.

Oh, Lord, what was happening to him? he wondered. He'd been divorced from Erica for five years, and not once since then had he allowed his thoughts to get wrapped up in a woman. Why would he want to put himself through that sort of misery again? If he wanted female company for the night, he knew where to find it. He certainly didn't have to start daydreaming about a mixed up, pregnant redhead. Yet there was something about her freshness and warm heart that was impossible for Jett to ignore.

The conflicting thoughts traipsing through his mind were suddenly interrupted as he caught the sounds of Bella entering the front door. Walter also heard her arrival and jumped off Jett's lap to race to the entryway to meet her.

"That damned cat is nothing but a traitor," Jett said to his sister, moments later, as she entered the room. "The minute he hears you're home, he leaves me."

Bella chuckled. "Walter isn't stupid. He knows who spoons out his food."

Jett rolled his eyes. "Yeah, and he apparently doesn't care who buys all those cans of tuna and salmon. I'm thinking it's about time Walter gets relegated to the barn."

"Hah. You've got the heart of a marshmallow. Before the night is over he'll be sleeping on the foot of your bed." Tossing her handbag and coat on the couch, Bella picked up the cat and carried him over to the fireplace. "The weather is getting worse and the heater in my car must be going on the blink. I froze all the way home."

"You should have stayed instead of trying to make the drive. Why didn't you spend the night with Mom?"

Bella stroked the cat, who'd already snuggled into a comfortable ball in her arms. "Because she has a houseguest. Trina, that old friend of hers from San Diego is visiting and I didn't want to be in the way. Besides, I figured Sassy might feel uncomfortable spending the night here alone with you."

Jett wondered what his sister would think if she knew just how obsessed he was becoming. If he confessed to kissing Sassy. If he told her he wanted to do it again. And again. Bella would probably tell him he'd lost his mind. And maybe he had, Jett thought.

Because there were a myriad of reasons he shouldn't get involved with Sassy.

He was thirty-two years old. She was far too young and inexperienced for him. Moreover, she was going to have a baby and he doubted the realities of motherhood and all that it entailed had completely sunk in with her. He didn't think he was ready to be a father, either. And then there was the search for her parents and the anchor those roots might give her. Trying to fit a man into her life right now wouldn't work. Besides, she deserved to have real love in her life. And Jett wasn't sure he believed in love anymore, much less that he was able to experience it.

"Sassy trusts me to be a gentleman," he said flatly. "Besides, she has other things besides me on her mind."

Bella leveled a curious look at him. "Oh, with all that was going on at Mom's today, I almost forgot. How did the meeting at the Silver Horn go this evening?"

Jett thrust a weary hand through his hair, then shook his head. "For starters, Bart took one look at Sassy and ordered us to leave the house."

Bella's eyes widened. "Are you kidding? I mean—I know I said he'd probably take one look at her and blow a gasket, but I didn't mean literally!"

He gestured toward a phone sitting on an end table. "Call Orin or one of the guys. They'll tell you. Bart behaved deplorably."

Moving away from the fireplace, Bella eased onto the edge of the couch and placed Walter on the cushion next to her. "What happened? Did you and Sassy leave?"

"She wanted to, and so did I. But before that could happen, Orin took hold of his father and ushered him out of the room. After that, everyone else was very cordial to Sassy and insisted that we stay. So we did. But Bart's absence was like an elephant sitting in the room."

The amazement on Bella's face grew even deeper. "Orin actually stepped up and took Bart out of the room? I've never known him to go against his father's wishes. I can't remember anybody in that family going against Bart. But since Claudia died, I've not been around the Calhouns all that much. Wow! That must've been quite a scene," she murmured thoughtfully.

Jett frowned. "Just imagine how Sassy must have felt, being ordered out of the house like that. If Bart was a few years younger I'd have knocked his fool head off," he muttered. "As it is, I'm wondering if the man is starting to suffer some sort of dementia."

Bella leveled a curious look at him. "So what do the rest of the family think about Sassy being related?"

He shrugged. "They batted around a few ideas, but none of them fit the puzzle. It's clear the brothers are clueless. But after Bart's reaction, I'm thinking something about Sassy's appearance scared him."

It was Bella's turn to frown. "Scared? You think that was the motive behind his behavior? I'm thinking he was just being his old, crotchety self. Otherwise, wouldn't he realize his behavior would cast a suspicious light on him?"

"Bart wasn't thinking clearly. He let his emotions grab hold of him before he thought about how he might sound or look to everyone. Sassy believes he reacted that way because she reminded him of Darci, the granddaughter that died."

"Hmm. Guess that's possible," Bella mused aloud. "Darci was a touchy subject with Claudia. The woman never offered to show me a picture of her late daughter or to talk about her. I guess the whole ordeal was just too painful for Claudia to deal with. Maybe it's the same with Bart, and the sight of Sassy did set him off."

"Well, Evan spoke right out and admitted that Sassy looked like their late sister. But the resemblance could all be coincidence and Bart is simply being like you suggested—old and crotchety."

Bella frowned. "This doesn't sound good, Jett. When you dig into any family there's always a chance you'll open a can of worms. Even if you're not worried about your job, you'd be alienating friends that you've had since childhood."

"Look, Bella, the old man was the only one raising a ruckus. I honestly believe the rest of the family would be pleased to discover that Sassy was a part of them, somehow."

"What about Orin? You haven't mentioned him in all of this."

Jett shrugged. "He was more than kind to Sassy. If he's hiding any sort of information, it certainly didn't show."

Bella rose to her feet. "There's always DNA testing, you know. Have you discussed that possibility with Sassy?"

"No. But it's crossed my mind more than once."

"Then why haven't you mentioned it to her?"

"Because I have the feeling she wouldn't want to go that route. To her that would be forcing the issue and she doesn't want to push herself on anyone." He swiped a hand over his face. "If the Calhouns suggested it, that might be different. But for now, Sassy believes everything is over. She wants to go home."

Ignoring the cat, Bella picked up her coat and handbag. "And you don't want her to go."

Sighing, he rose to his feet and walked over to the fireplace. Bella was right, he thought. He didn't want Sassy to go. At least, not yet. Her spunky courage and generous smile made her so different from his ex-wife that being in her company almost made him forget he'd sworn off women. Not to mention that he still couldn't get that impulsive kiss out of his mind.

As he pulled the screen shut, he said, "If she's a Calhoun she deserves to be acknowledged as one."

"And the fact that you like her has nothing to do with your wanting to keep her here."

Turning, he frowned at his sister. "Is anything wrong with that?"

She answered with a knowing smile. "You

should be asking yourself that question, not me." Suddenly yawning, she covered her open mouth with her hand. "Sorry, Jett. I'm dog tired. I'll see you in the morning."

As Jett watched his sister leave the room, he realized Bella was right. He needed to ask himself several things regarding his feelings toward Sassy. Trouble was, he didn't know if he could find the answers.

Early the next morning, after spending a fitful night rolling from one side of his bed to the other, Jett entered the kitchen to find Sassy sitting at the table dressed in a robe and pajamas with a cup of coffee in front of her. A cell phone was jammed to her ear and what she was saying stopped him in his tracks.

"Oh, so, not today? Then tomorrow is the first flight with an open seat? What time will it be departing?"

Before he could stop himself or even think about what he was doing, Jett leaned across the table, plucked the phone from her hand and ended the call.

Incredulous, Sassy leaped to her feet and grabbed at the phone he had clutched in his fist. "Give me that!" she ordered. "I was trying to make my flight arrangements! You've broken the connection!"

He lifted the phone even farther out of her reach, and with a wail of frustration she jumped and snatched at his hand in an attempt to retrieve it. Her effort not only failed, but caused her to teeter forward and fall against his chest.

Before she could manage to right herself, Jett wrapped his arms around her and tugged her even closer. "That was my intention," he said lowly. "To keep you here."

Her head lolled backward, and as he watched a look of surprise part her plush lips, nothing about the Calhouns or why she'd come to Nevada mattered. All he could think about was tasting those lips again, of feeling her warm curves pressed close to him.

Their gazes locked and the soft lights flickering in her eyes drew his head down to hers.

"Jett."

His whispered name was little more than a soft breath brushing his cheeks and the erotic sensation broke the last tenuous thread of his self-control.

With a groan vibrating deep in his throat, he tightened the circle of his arms and closed the last bit of space between their mouths.

Jett never planned for the kiss to get out of control, but after the first few seconds of having her in his arms, his ability to think vanished and the more basic senses of taste and touch took over.

Her lips were like a rich dessert. One that he'd not allowed himself to indulge in for far too long. And the hunger her kiss invoked in him was swiftly taking control. As his lips feasted on the sweet curves of her mouth, he could feel the warmth of her hands lying flat against his shoulders, the soft mounds of her breasts pressing against his chest.

He didn't want the pleasure to end, but far too soon she began to stir and draw away. Jett forced himself to lift his head and allow her to step back and out of his arms.

While he sucked in a deep breath and tried to gather his senses, she swallowed hard and shoved a swathe of hair off her forehead. "What was that supposed to be?" she finally asked. "Some sort of persuasion to make me stay?"

His gaze took in her powder-blue robe and silky white pajamas, the red hair curling wild and free upon her shoulders and the naked curve of her just-kissed lips. He couldn't remember any woman ever looking more desirable to him, and the urge to pull her back into his arms stirred like a churning sea in the pit of his stomach.

"I don't know," he answered frankly. "Could it? Persuade you, I mean?"

Her lips pressed together as a shade of deep coral flooded her cheeks.

"No! It's shown me that the sooner I get out of here, the better!"

"Why?" he asked softly. "You seemed to be enjoying that kiss as much as I was."

Turning her back to him, she sank into the chair she'd been sitting in when he first entered the kitchen. She was clearly stunned, but then, so was he. Grabbing her phone, then snatching her into his arms wasn't his normal behavior. But when he'd heard her making plans to leave, his first reaction was to stop her. For her sake and for his.

"That's exactly why I need to go," she murmured in a voice so low he could hardly hear it. "I might be tempted to kiss you again. And that wouldn't be good."

Moving up behind her, he gently placed a hand on her shoulder. "Sassy, I understand you've been through a lot lately, and I'm probably not helping matters, kissing you that way. But that doesn't mean you're supposed to turn off your feelings as a woman."

Beneath his fingers, he could feel her body stiffen.

"I've got to do that," she said flatly. "I'm going to have a baby."

The confusion in her voice had Jett groaning with frustration. "Does that mean you're going to shut yourself off? To never allow another man into your life? That's not normal, Sassy."

"Maybe not. But I'm not taking chances. At least…not for a long time."

Sighing, he placed her phone on the table near her coffee cup. If she wanted to leave that badly, there was nothing he could do about it.

"I can't blame you for feeling that way," he admitted. "For a long time now, I've not wanted to take chances. But I—for a moment there with you—well, I almost wanted to."

Her head suddenly swiveled around and the questions he saw in her eyes had him quickly turning and walking over to the kitchen cabinets. Jett wasn't ready to explain the heartache he'd gone through any more than he was ready to explain what he was feeling at the moment. Mainly because he wasn't exactly sure what he was feeling.

"Jett, I don't think…"

Her words trailed away on a wary note and he decided the best thing he could do for the both of them right now was to focus her attention on the Calhouns and away from that impulsive kiss. "Forget about me and that kiss, Sassy. And forget about hurrying back to New Mexico. It's far too soon for you to be calling this quits with the Calhouns."

As he fetched a cup from the cabinet, he darted a glance in her direction. She was frowning at him with sheer disbelief.

"The Calhouns? I thought lawyers were supposed to have common sense. Clearly you missed out on your share of it."

He shoved the cup under the coffee machine and punched the brew button. "You're probably right. Common sense would tell me to let you run back to New Mexico with your tail tucked between your legs. But my gut instinct is telling me that you should stay here. Until you learn for sure whether you have a connection to the Calhoun family."

The stream of coffee gurgled to a stop and Jett carried the cup over to the table. As he sank into the chair angled to her left, she looked at him, and the sight of her blue eyes and fresh young face had him suddenly wondering how it would feel to have her with him every morning, to have the right to kiss her and make love to her. Would it be different with Sassy? Would it be tender togetherness? Or the constant nightmare he'd endured with Erica?

"Jett, I told you from the very beginning—"

Her words were suddenly interrupted by the ringing of his phone sitting on the end of the breakfast bar. Jett excused himself and went to answer it.

As soon as he spotted the name on the caller ID, a sense of unease rushed through him. No one at the Silver Horn called him early on a Sunday morning. Yanking up the receiver, he answered briskly, "Jett here."

"Jett, it's Orin. I hate to bother you so early, but I thought you ought to know that Dad is in the hospital."

Jett glanced anxiously over at Sassy. Oh, God, she was already concerned about causing trouble for the family. What was she going to think now? he wondered sickly. "What happened?"

"His blood pressure went out of sight. The

doctor is trying to get it under control before he suffers a stroke."

"I'm sorry to hear this, Orin. Especially after last night. Bart wasn't happy about something."

"Hell, Jett, don't blame this on your visit last night. We both know that Dad has had problems with his blood pressure these past few years. And his temper. And the two don't mix well."

Jett had known Bart Calhoun from the time he'd been a young boy. He'd even considered the man as an extended grandfather. But he'd always been aware of Bart's hot head and domineering ways. Some men mellowed with age. Unfortunately, Bart had done the opposite and grown even more ornery.

"Bart isn't the most laid-back person in the world," Jett agreed, then asked, "Is there anything I can do?"

"Thanks, but there's nothing right now. I'll keep you informed."

By the time Jett hung up the phone, Sassy was already on her feet, walking toward him. "I wasn't trying to eavesdrop," she said, "but I couldn't help overhearing something about the hospital. What's happened?"

Seeing no way to soften the news, he didn't

hedge. "It's Bart. He's in the hospital being treated for dangerously high blood pressure."

Stunned by the news, Sassy's hand clutched her throat. "Oh, my. This is just awful, Jett. So awful."

He touched fingertips to her cheek. "You've gone very pale, Sassy. And I don't want this to upset you."

"But it does! You saw the man last night. The sight of me sent him into a rage. My coming here has made him ill!"

Wrapping his hands around her shoulders, he said, "If the sight of you has affected Bart this much, then it's clear he's covering for someone or himself. And I'm going to find out what it's all about."

Dropping her head in her hands, she moaned with misgivings. "Nothing is worth this, Jett. If Bart Calhoun dies—"

"He isn't going to die! The old man is too tough and stubborn to do that. But clearly his health will have to get better before I can talk to him about this. That's why you can't get in a hurry to leave."

"But it would be best for everyone if I did," she argued.

"Really? You came here hoping to find information about your parents. But I think you want to leave, not because of the Calhouns or Bart, but because of me."

Removing her hands from her face, she looked at him through squinted eyes. "If you're referring to that kiss—"

"That's exactly what I'm referring to."

"Sorry to deflate your ego," she said with defiant sarcasm. "But you didn't exactly shake the ground beneath my feet."

Undeterred by her flippant reply, his hands slipped from her shoulders to her back. "Then maybe I should try again," he murmured.

Wide-eyed, she wriggled away from him and rushed out of the room just as Bella was entering it.

"What's wrong with her?" Bella asked as she stared after Sassy's retreating back.

Swiping a hand through his hair, Jett walked over to the refrigerator and began to collect bacon, eggs and butter in the crook of his arm. "I'll tell you about it over breakfast."

A half hour later, Sassy had dressed in jeans and a dark green shirt and was straightening the bedcovers when a knock sounded on the door.

Expecting it to be Jett, she was surprised

and somewhat relieved when she opened the door to see Bella standing in front of her.

"May I come in?" she asked politely.

"Please do." Sassy opened the door wider. "I was just tidying the bed."

"I hope you've been comfortable," Bella said, as she walked past Sassy into the spacious bedroom.

Walking over to the bed, Sassy finished smoothing the thick white comforter. "Everything is very nice, Bella. To be honest, I'm not used to sleeping in such luxury. In my little rental I only have enough space for a twin bed, and the mattress on it is beginning to sag."

Bella took a seat on the cedar chest located at the foot of the bed. "So you don't room with the family you work for?"

Walking over to the dresser, Sassy picked up a yellow-and-green scarf and looped it loosely around her neck. "I did when I first went to work for them. Back then I was only a teenager with no other place to go."

"Jett told me about the fire that took your parents and your home. I can't begin to imagine going through such tragedy."

Even though her gaze was on the mirror, Sassy wasn't really seeing herself. She was seeing George and Gloria Matthews, the two people she'd believed had been responsible for bringing her into this world. Now all the wonderful memories she had of her adoptive parents were skewed with confusion and even a sense of betrayal. She'd always been a strong girl. She could have handled the truth. But maybe they'd not seen that strength in her. Or perhaps they'd simply wanted to shield her from her uncertain beginnings. Either way, she'd never have the chance to ask them why they'd withheld the truth from her.

"The Cantrells got me through it," she told Bella. "And when I turned twenty I decided it was time for me to find a place of my own."

Bella asked, "You like living on your own better?"

Turning away from the dresser, Sassy shrugged. "Most of the time I like having my privacy. Other times it can get pretty lonely."

"I understand exactly. Before Jett talked me into moving in with him I was living alone. I'm divorced," Bella explained.

Bella was a beautiful and intelligent woman. Sassy couldn't imagine any man allowing her to slip out of his life, but then Bella could be the one who'd initiated the divorce. Either way, Sassy wasn't going to pry.

"I'm sorry things didn't work out for you," she told Bella.

With a wry smile, the other woman waved a dismissive hand through the air. "I was sorry, too—when it happened. But that's all in the past. Right now, I want to make sure you're okay. Jett says you've not eaten breakfast yet."

"There wasn't any need for him to send you to check on me," Sassy said with a spurt of annoyance.

Bella's brows rose to a faint arch. "He didn't. He's already eaten and left the house to go feed the livestock. I was the one who was worried about you eating."

Sassy let out a pent-up breath. The mere fact that Jett was no longer in the house was enough to leave her feeling unexplainably empty. Heaven help her! Was it the pregnancy causing an overload of hormones to make her crazy? Or just the power of the man himself? When she was near him, she was constantly telling herself that she needed to run from the excitement and pleasure he made her feel. Then, when she was away from him, she wanted to be right back in his arms.

She said, "Oh. Well, thanks for asking. But actually I'm not feeling very hungry."

Rising from her seat on the chest, Bella walked over to where Sassy stood. "I'm hardly an expert on the subject, but shouldn't you be eating for the baby now? I've heard the first few months of nutrition are the most important. Maybe you could handle some toast and juice? It might make you feel better."

Bella's suggestions were enough to make Sassy see she was behaving immaturely, and that was worse than embarrassing. She was a responsible woman with a baby on the way. She needed to be behaving that way instead of letting Jett's kiss turn her into a silly schoolgirl.

"Bella, I'm sorry. Normally I'm not so—"

"Emotional?" Bella suggested with an understanding smile.

"You're being kind to call it that," Sassy said ruefully. "And you're right about breakfast. I have to eat for my baby now. Not just myself."

Bella gave her shoulder a reassuring pat. "Don't beat yourself up, Sassy. So much has been going on since you got here that your head has to be in a mixed-up whirl. And now Jett tells me that Bart has been hospitalized and you're feeling somewhat guilty about it."

"Feeling guilty is putting it mildly," Sassy admitted.

"That's hogwash. You've done nothing to the man. So don't fret about it." She nudged Sassy toward the door. "Come on. Let's eat and then I thought we'd drive into town and do some shopping."

Sassy shot her a blank look. "Shopping?"

Bella chuckled. "Yes, shopping. I need to pick up a few things before I go to work tomorrow. I thought you might like to look around and see what Carson City has to offer. You don't need maternity clothes yet, but you will pretty soon. You might find something on sale. Besides, I want to be the first one to buy the baby a gift."

"You're too nice, Bella. And yes, it would be fun. Thanks for asking."

Spending the day with Bella, shopping for the baby and seeing Carson City would be far better than moping around here, fretting about Bart and dreading the time she would have to board a plane that would take her back to New Mexico and away from Jett Sundell.

You came here searching for your family. But I think you want to leave because of me.

As she and Bella walked to the kitchen, Jett's words continued to drift through her mind. He had it wrong, she thought dismally. She didn't want to leave. She wanted to stay here and enjoy his company, to let herself believe that something real and strong could develop between them.

But that would be like letting herself believe in fairy tales. And even fairy tales had to come to an end. Didn't they?

Chapter 6

The next morning Jett was walking back from the barn when the sound of a vehicle caught his attention. Pausing on the hard-packed earth, he glanced around to see a pickup truck rising over the crest in the road. From the dark blue color, he knew it was a Silver Horn ranch truck, so he waited for it to pull alongside him.

When the driver's-side window slid down, Finn Calhoun appeared behind the wheel. He was dressed in cowboy work gear, including a dark burgundy scarf wrapped around his neck and secured tightly with a band of braided rawhide. In spite of looking unusually tired, there was a friendly smile on his face.

"Morning, Jett. You headed toward the house or the barn?"

"The house. With the snow starting to fall again, I thought I'd get my feeding chores done early. What brings you out?"

"If you've got the time to spare I have something to show you and Sassy. She's still here, isn't she?"

"She is." But for how long, Jett didn't know. She'd spent the whole day with Bella yesterday, and last night she'd purposely avoided being alone with him. She'd not mentioned anything about her plans to book a flight, and each time he'd even tried to head the conversation in the direction of her plans, Bella had jumped in and steered it to another track.

"Go park," Jett told him. "We'll go through the back door."

Moments later, the two men walked across the ranch yard to the house until they reached a small, screened-in back porch. The dogs followed them and quickly ducked into a doghouse sitting a few steps away from the door.

"Damn, but I don't like this cold," Finn said as he stomped his boots and brushed at the snow that had collected on his oiled duster.

"Better get used to it," he said. "Winter isn't half over yet." Jett made an attempt to rid himself of the white stuff, then opened the door and motioned Finn into the house.

Inside the kitchen, the two men deposited their hats and jackets on a coatrack, then Jett gestured toward a small breakfast bar that created an L shape at the end of the cabinets. "Have a seat, Finn, and I'll get us some coffee. I'm not sure if Sassy is up yet. Maybe she'll show in a few minutes."

Finn made himself comfortable on one of the wooden barstools while Jett went to work preparing the coffee.

"Any news about your grandfather?" Jett asked. "I've not heard anything else from your father."

"He's doing a bit better, I think. After I leave here, I plan to drive to the hospital and check on him."

"That's encouraging news. Maybe he'll get to go home soon."

Finn grimaced. "I'm not so sure that's a good idea. When he's on the ranch, you can't slow him down. He wants to oversee everything. As far as he's concerned, I've still not learned what to do with a horse. Even though

I manage the ranch's remuda and broodmare production," he added sardonically.

"Bart is just Bart," Jett reasoned as he carried two steaming mugs of coffee over to the bar. "But I'll be honest with you, Finn, that behavior of his the other night was bizarre."

Grimacing, Finn stirred a dollop of cream into his coffee. "Yeah, he embarrassed the hell out of all of us with that outburst."

"He also hurt Sassy. That's what I hated about it."

Finn glanced ruefully at him. "We're all sorry about that, Jett. If we'd had any idea he was going to pull such a stunt we would have warned you."

"No matter. It's done. I expect Sassy to be leaving soon. Maybe even tomorrow." And the idea of never seeing her, touching her again was eating a hole right through him. From the very first day he'd met Sassy, he'd been telling himself over and over not to get involved. But with each passing day she continued to surprise and enchant him. It was too soon to give her up. Way too soon.

"No!" Finn blurted, the cup pausing halfway to his lips. "She can't do that!"

Jett's eyes narrowed on the younger man. "Why?"

"Because I— We—"

Finn's words broke off abruptly as he lifted his gaze to a point above Jett's shoulder. Following the other man's gaze, Jett looked around to see Sassy entering the room. To his relief, she wasn't wearing her bedclothes as she had been yesterday morning. Instead, she was dressed in a pair of black corduroys and a red sweater that draped low against her chest. The color of the fabric made her thick hair look like a copper blaze and her skin a smooth shell pink.

The moment she spotted Jett and Finn at the bar, she stopped in her tracks and stared fearfully at them.

"What's wrong? Is Mr. Calhoun worse?" she asked in a rush.

"No. He's doing better," Jett quickly reassured her. "Come have coffee. Finn has something he wants to show us."

While Sassy prepared herself a cup of decaffeinated coffee and loaded it with cream and sugar, she tried not to let curiosity over Finn's appearance lead to hope about finding her real parents. Especially since she'd been convincing herself that it was time to go home.

With coffee in hand, she walked over to where the two men sat at the breakfast bar, and though everything inside of her wanted to sidle up to Jett, she forced herself to stand a respectable distance away from him.

"Morning, Sassy," Finn said with a warm smile. "You're looking beautiful this morning—in spite of resembling me."

She laughed softly. "Thank you, Finn. It's nice to see you again."

"Jett tells me you're thinking about flying home soon. Is that true?"

She darted a wary glance at Jett. After that kiss they'd shared yesterday morning, all sorts of emotions and questions had been pushing and shoving their way into her thoughts. And the only sure thing she'd been able to take from any of them was that Jett made her feel things she'd never experienced in her life. Special things that made her heart feel warm and full, her pulse beat with excitement. If she ran back to New Mexico now, she might never know if a real relationship could build between them. Losing that chance might even be worse than never finding her biological parents.

"I— To tell you the truth, Finn, I've not yet decided when to go home. My boss thinks I need a little vacation. She wants me to stay and visit Lake Tahoe, so I'm thinking I might do that before I head back to New Mexico."

Was that a look of relief she saw flicker across Jett's face? She couldn't be sure about him, but it was clear her reply had pleased Finn.

"Great! That's just great, because me and my brothers have been talking it over and we think there's something going on with our grandfather. After you and Jett left the other night, Dad pressed him on the issue of you being related to the family and he, well, exploded. He cursed us for doubting his honesty and for being ungrateful—as though none of us have ever turned a hand to a day of work in our lives. He's insulted us all. That's what he's done. Besides making himself look mighty suspicious."

"Finn, your grandfather probably assumed that I had plans to insert myself into his family," Sassy said, "and he reacted defensively. That's understandable."

"I've already had this argument with her," Jett told Finn. "She's hard to convince."

"Maybe this will help." Reaching for his shirt pocket, Finn opened the flap and pulled out a small envelope. "Dad doesn't know I took this from Mom's things. And I don't know whether he'd be mad about it or not. But that doesn't matter. This is too important to me and my brothers."

Sassy instinctively moved closer to Jett's side as Finn opened the envelope and placed a small photo on the bar top.

"This was my sister, Darci. I think it was taken around the time she turned two. That would make it a few months before she died."

As Sassy studied the image captured on the glossy square of paper, goose bumps rushed over her skin. "Oh, my! I think both of you should see something. Wait just a minute."

She rushed to her bedroom, dug a pair of small snapshots from one of her suitcases, then hurried back to the kitchen.

Placing the photos in front of the two men, she said, "I brought these with me, just in case someone might be interested. These were among a few things that survived the fire. I was about three years old when these were taken. A little older than Darci was in her photo, but we do resemble each other."

"It's uncanny how much you look like her," Jett murmured.

"Oh, wow! Can I take one of these to show my brothers?" Finn asked her.

"Certainly. I'm not sure what it could mean, but—"

Finn interrupted, "It means we need to get the ball rolling."

"How do you expect to do that?" Jett asked. "You brothers are clueless and Bart isn't talking."

Finn grimaced. "That's why I—we brothers—think we need to do DNA testing."

Finn's suggestion made Sassy's queasy stomach take a crazy tumble. "Oh, Finn! Have you and your brothers thought about this? The damage it might cause with your grandfather!"

Finn looked from her to Jett, then back to her. "We've talked it over and we're willing to take the chance. We're not little boys anymore. One way or the other, we have a right to know the truth."

Jett's arm settled against the back of her waist. "What do you think about this, Sassy? Surely the idea has crossed your mind before now."

"Sure, I've considered the idea. DNA is the first thing people want to turn to whenever there are doubts about parentage, crimes and everything in between. It could prove whether I have some relationship to the Calhouns. But what good would that do if I didn't know who was responsible for my birth or why I was given away?"

"If you're a close enough relative," Finn argued, "that would be enough to force the truth to surface. Whatever it might be."

Without even realizing it, she reached for the comfort of Jett's hand. When his fingers closed around hers, it prompted her gaze to connect with his.

"You don't like that word, 'force,' do you?" he asked gently.

"Not one bit," she said with a sigh, then looked at Finn. Could the handsome rancher and his brothers possibly be some part of her family? The idea was incredible and yet she was beginning to believe it might be possible. "Me doing a DNA test is only going to make your grandfather view me as a gold digger. And I can hardly blame him. Wouldn't it be better if the truth was revealed by a member of the family, not by some data produced in a laboratory?"

Frustrated with her cautious attitude, Finn swiped a hand over his face. "Of course, it would be much better. But Granddad has pushed the mute button, and the condition of his health right now makes it impossible for us to press him about the issue. As for Dad, we honestly don't believe he's deliberately keeping anything from us. He seems as baffled about this as we are."

"Wait just a minute, Finn," Jett interrupted. "What I'd like to know is exactly why you brothers are so all-fired anxious to prove Sassy is a Calhoun. Do you honestly want her to be some relation? Or are you just using it as an excuse to challenge your high-handed grandfather?"

Finn rolled his eyes toward the ceiling. "Hell, Jett, you sound just like a lawyer."

"He is a lawyer," Sassy reminded him. "Your family's lawyer. Did you forget?"

The redheaded horseman gave Sassy a lopsided grin. "No. But sometimes it does momentarily slip my mind. I don't know if Jett's told you, but he pretty much grew up with us. He's close to the same age as my oldest brother, Clancy. We all went to the same school and share many of the same friends. He's Jett to me. Not just the person who handles our legal affairs."

"Well, friend or lawyer, Jett's question is exactly what I've been wondering, too. Why are you and your brothers pushing this matter?" Sassy asked.

His expression suddenly solemn, Finn touched a finger to the edge of Darci's photo. "This has nothing to do with Grandfather. Sure, me and my brothers get angry as heck with him, but that doesn't mean we'd ever want to exact some sort of revenge. This is about, well... We lost our only sister. You can't replace her, Sassy, but having you in the family sure would be a nice second chance for us."

Tears misted Sassy's eyes, and her voice came out low and hoarse. "Finn—I—I don't know what to say. I never expected you or your brothers might feel this way."

The tightening of Jett's hand around hers, pulled her gaze around to his face, and the tender light she saw in his brown eyes caused her heart to swell and the mist in her eyes to turn to all-out tears.

"Just because someone gave you away twenty-four years ago doesn't mean you're not wanted now," he said softly.

She tried to smile but her quivering lips made it impossible. "Thank you for saying that, Jett."

The intimate connection between her and Jett stretched on and on until Finn finally cleared his throat and reminded them there was a third person in the room.

Her cheeks flushed, Sassy turned away from Jett and looked to Finn. "Okay, I'll do the DNA test," she told him. "As long as everyone understands that this has nothing to do with property or inheritance or anything of that sort. I don't want anything of monetary value. All I want is the truth about who I am. Understand?"

A wide grin spread across Finn's face. "Great, Sassy. We were all hoping you'd agree." He looked at Jett. "Evan says we need a legal DNA test done—one that will stand up in court. So that means we can't use a home do-it-yourself kit. We need to go to the health department in town. They have technicians who can take samples, and the lab they use is one of the best in the country. If you can have Sassy there on Monday morning, I'll meet you two there."

"So, you're going to be the donor for your family?" Jett asked him.

Finn nodded. "I'm the one who got this whole thing started. I'll do whatever is needed to see it through."

"Okay. I'll have her there by nine. If we

can't make it for some reason, I'll call," Jett assured him.

"Good. Then I'll see you two Monday." Finn gave Jett a grateful slap on the shoulder, then turned to Sassy and reached for her hand. But rather than shake it, he used it to pull her close enough to place a quick kiss on her cheek.

The unexpected show of affection took Sassy by complete surprise, and from the look on Jett's face it had surprised him, too.

"Hey, is that supposed to be a sisterly kiss?" Jett asked with annoyance.

Chuckling, Finn started to the door. "What other kind would it be?"

They watched him leave the house before Jett slowly turned to Sassy.

"So Finn succeeded where I failed," he said wryly.

"What do you mean?"

He slanted her a challenging glance. "He talked you into staying. I couldn't seem to do it."

Sassy had no idea when Bella might walk into the kitchen, but for the moment she was acutely aware that she and Jett were completely alone. Slipping her arms around his waist would be so heavenly, she thought. But it would be a mistake to initiate an embrace with this man. Especially when she was smart enough to know that one kiss wouldn't satisfy the desire growing deep inside her. No, she'd want more and more. As for Jett, she wasn't yet sure of what he wanted from her. But she had a feeling he was soon going to show her.

With a nervous lick of her lips, she said, "He gave me a specific reason to stay."

His green eyes locked on to hers. "I guess that means my reason wasn't specific enough," he murmured.

"Jett," she said ruefully, "if you're still talking about that kiss, I— Well, just because I've agreed to stay on here in your house doesn't mean I feel obligated to give in to your— urgings."

"Your being in my house has nothing to do with it. I never want you to feel obligated to me." He wrapped his hands around her upper arms. "I'm talking about the tremble I felt on your lips—the hunger I tasted there. If you want to pretend that you didn't feel anything when I had you in my arms, then go ahead. But I'm not going to lie to you or myself about it. I wanted to make love to you."

Make love. The soft, caressing way he spoke

those two words punctured the flimsy wall of resistance she'd tried to erect between them.

"Don't you mean you wanted to have sex with me?"

He cupped his palm against the side of her face. "If it's easier for you to deal with that, then call it sex."

The rapid thud of her heart was causing the thin fabric of her sweater to flutter against her breasts. Did he see it? Did he have any idea how much she was trembling inside?

"None of this—whatever is happening between us—is easy, Jett. I'm trying to use common sense, but you expect me to throw caution to the wind and behave as if there's no tomorrow. I did that with Barry. I won't be that reckless again."

"I'm not Barry," he reminded her. "I'm older and hopefully wiser."

"That's right. That makes you even more of a risk than he was. Because it's obvious you're a man who's sworn off love."

His eyes narrowed. "Where did you get that?"

With a troubled groan, she started to step around him. "I'm hungry. I'm going to make myself some breakfast."

He gently but firmly drew her back to him.

"We'll eat in a few minutes. Right now I want you to explain that remark. Has Bella been talking about me?"

She glowered at him. "Not hardly! If I wanted to know something personal about you, I'd ask you. Not anyone else."

He blew out a heavy breath. "Something made you form that opinion about me. What was it?"

"You don't have a girlfriend or a wife," she reasoned. "And I get the feeling that you don't want any woman on a permanent basis. I think you like living alone. Without anyone to answer to."

Suddenly the back of his fingers were gently rubbing her cheek and desire flooded the deepest part of her.

"Have you ever thought that I might live alone, because I've not found another woman I want to live with?"

She breathed deeply as she fought to hang on to her rattled senses. "Whatever your reason, it doesn't matter. I can't allow myself to have an affair with you."

One of his dark brows arched with speculation. "Who said I wanted an affair?"

He was a lawyer. She was a maid. What else could he want, Sassy asked herself, except a quick romp between the sheets? "Well, whatever you're asking for, I can't give it to you."

To her surprise a slight smile lifted the corners of his lips.

"I'm not asking you for anything, Sassy. At least, not yet."

She was trying to summon enough courage to ask him what he meant by that, when he put a hand on her shoulder and nudged her toward the working area of the kitchen.

"Come on," he said. "Let's cook breakfast. I'm starving."

That afternoon, the weather worsened and Jett called his hired hand in to help him haul an extra load of hay out to the cattle. As the truck slipped and spun over the dirt track, Jett wrestled with the steering wheel while Noah braced a hand on the dashboard.

The ranch hand glanced over at Jett. "You worried about the storm or something? You've been awfully quiet."

"Sorry, Noah, I'm not good company today. But it's not the storm worrying me. This nasty weather will probably blow out in the next day or two. I have a lot on my mind, that's all."

Like a perky redhead with honey-sweet lips, Jett thought. Now that she'd agreed to hang around for a while longer, he wondered how he was going to keep his hands off her. And why would he want to, when touching her made him feel more alive than he'd felt in years?

I can't allow myself to have an affair with you.

Something about her words had stung him on several different levels. She believed the only thing he wanted was to take her to bed and she was partially right. So why should that bother him? Because it wasn't all about sex. And that troubling fact continued to nag at him.

"Yesterday in the coffee shop I heard about old man Calhoun being in the hospital. Is it serious?"

Jett glanced over at Noah, The big, brawny guy was only a couple of years older than Jett's thirty-two, but the soulful depth of his dark eyes made him seem much older. It was no secret that some folks considered Noah a drifter who lacked ambition. Some had even warned Jett that he was asking for trouble by letting Noah live in a small cabin on the edge of the J Bar S, but Jett ignored the talk.

As far as he was concerned, he'd trust Noah with his life.

"I talked with Orin about an hour ago, and he says his father is better. The doctor plans to keep him hospitalized for a while longer, though."

After a long, thoughtful moment, Noah said, "Poor old man. He's so busy worrying about losing the things he has that he doesn't have time to stop and enjoy them."

Was that the real problem with Bart? Did he already know that Sassy was a Calhoun and was concerned that she could take the family to the cleaners? Normally that would be a question anyone would take to their family lawyer. But Bart clearly wasn't seeking Jett's advice this time. Which could only mean that the old man considered Jett too close to Sassy to be able to confide in him. A fact that was going to make it even harder for Jett to discover the truth. Something he'd like to do long before the DNA results were revealed.

Trying to put a halt to his meandering thoughts, Jett said, "Yeah. Sometimes I think it would be a nightmare to be as rich as Bart Calhoun."

Noah let out a humorous grunt. "That's one problem I'll never have to worry about."

"Oh, I wouldn't say that," Jett joked. "You might decide to take up panning and hit the mother lode."

"That's about as likely as me getting married. And there's no chance in hell of that ever happening."

The sarcastic remark had Jett glancing over at the other man, but he didn't make any sort of reply. Noah was prickly about discussing his personal life and Jett never pushed the issue. As long as Noah did the work he asked of him, Jett was only too happy to respect his privacy.

"I should tell you, just in case you see her around the barn or the house that I—that is, Bella and I, have a house guest."

Noah turned a curious look on him. "She? You have a woman in the house? Besides your sister?"

Jett frowned. "You say that like she's a case of chicken pox or mumps."

The hired hand shrugged one shoulder. "I'm just surprised, that's all. I don't remember you ever having much company. She a relative or something?"

"No. She's from New Mexico. She came

out here looking for a clue to her biological parents. It's a long story, Noah, but in a nutshell, there's a chance she might be related to the Calhouns. That's how I got involved. And that's why my mind is about to burst. I really don't know how all of this is going to play out or exactly how I should go about dealing with it."

"Hmm. Just tell me one thing, Jett, is this woman young and pretty or a wrinkled grandma?"

"Young and pretty. And…pregnant."

The last word brought a faint arch to one of Noah's brows. "Oh. So you're safe. She's a married woman."

"No. Single."

Noah grunted. "There has to be a daddy hanging around somewhere."

Jett grimaced. "No again. He's dead. A rodeo accident."

That brought Noah's head around. "Aw, heck. That's tough."

"That's only one of the rough spots Sassy's had in her life."

"And you feel sorry for her."

Did he? Jett asked himself. No. He believed she deserved better in life. But she was too capable and spunky to feel sorry for. The morning he'd taken Sassy with him on his feeding rounds, and she'd talked about the cattle and having a ranch of her own someday, he'd been more than surprised. He'd not expected her to know anything about ranching, much less desire that type of life. And though most people would probably laugh at her dreams, he respected her for believing she could achieve them.

"So far, she has my admiration, not my sympathy. And I would like to see good things come into her life."

Noah solemnly shook his head. "God help you. That's all I have to say about it."

A wry grimace twisted Jett's features. "What? No sage advice? No warnings?"

Noah's chuckle held little humor. "You're all grown up. You've been through the hearth, home and wife thing. I don't need to give you advice." He turned his attention to the passenger window and suddenly barked out, "Put on the brakes! You've missed the turnoff to the north pasture."

Cursing under his breath, Jett stomped on the brakes, then jerked the gearshift into reverse. "It's this damned snow. I can't see where I'm going."

"Yeah," Noah said with sarcasm. "It's the snow that's got you blinded."

Chapter 7

Later that night, after the evening meal, Bella left for Carson City to meet up with a friend and take in a movie. Bella had been kind enough to invite Sassy to join her, but she'd politely declined. Now, as she watched Jett throw another log on the fire, she was trying to figure out how she could retire to her room and not make it look as though she was running from his company.

"You don't like going to the movies?" he asked, as he finished levering the log into place with a poker. "I thought you'd jump at the chance to go with Bella and get away from here for a few hours."

"Normally I would have jumped at the chance. I love to go out and enjoy myself." From her seat on the couch, Sassy kicked off her ankle boots and curled her feet beneath her. "But I guess the traveling and everything is catching up with me. I'm feeling a little tired."

Striding over to the couch, he eased down on the opposite end, and even though three feet of space separated them, it felt like three inches to Sassy.

"You're not getting sick, are you?"

The faint annoyance on his face made her wonder if he was already considering her a burden.

"There's no need for you to concern yourself," she answered more crisply than she'd intended. "I am pregnant, and the doctor said I'll probably be feeling more fatigued than usual. I've been reading up a bit—I got a book when Bella and I were out shopping. But all seems good. I'll know more when I'm back home and get a full workup from my doctor."

"Well, I don't know anything about the health issues of pregnant women. But you've had a lot to deal with these past few days.

And this morning—that photo of Darci had to be shocking to you. It was to me."

The photo had knocked her for a loop, all right, Sassy thought. But Jett's kiss was the thing she couldn't push from her mind. He didn't need to know that—she'd already shown the man just how attracted she was to him. There wasn't any need to remind him of the fact, she thought ruefully.

"The photo got to me," she admitted. "When I was a child I would look at old family photos that my adopted parents stored in a big shoe box. I didn't resemble anybody in those photos, and whenever I'd ask my parents who I looked like in the family they'd always laugh and say I had a look all my own."

"Hmm. Guess that was a gentle way to put it."

"They were lying to me." With a shake of her head, she turned her gaze to the fireplace. "That's the part that hurts the most. Still, I cherish those years I had them in my life. I was happy growing up. And sometimes I even feel as though I'm betraying George and Gloria by searching for my real parents." Closing her eyes, she pressed fingertips to her forehead. "I'm causing an awful stir in the

Calhoun family. And I keep asking myself if any of this is worth the knowing."

He scooted over two empty cushions until he was at her side, and when he reached for her hand Sassy trembled with anticipation.

"Sassy, I realize I've been pushing you about this. But it's only because I believe that, in the long run, you'll be happier. Whether it turns out that you belong to the Calhoun family or some other family. Your search will have to go on until you find the truth. Otherwise, you'll continue to carry around questions and doubts."

She studied his rugged face and wondered what might have happened if the two of them had crossed paths under different circumstances. Would he have noticed her? Somehow she doubted it, but she would've definitely looked his way and tried her best to catch his attention. Now she was different. Now she realized that actually loving a man was far different than simply dating him and enjoying his company.

"I can tell you I'm not a bit happy that the Calhoun brothers are conspiring behind their grandfather's back."

"Conspiring? That's a pretty harsh way of putting things."

His thumb slid slowly and surely against the back of her hand, and the seductive motion was making it impossible for Sassy to concentrate on his words.

"I didn't mean to sound harsh," she mumbled. "But they are keeping things from him. And that's equally bad."

"Like hell," he cursed. "You ought to be happy they want you to be a part of the family."

Easing her hand from his, she rose from the couch and walked over to the picture window that framed a view of the front yard. Darkness shrouded the tall pines, but a nearby yard lamp shed enough light to illuminate the falling snow and the drifts accumulating against the fat tree trunks.

"If their family is torn apart by all this they won't be happy. But it's too late to worry about it now. I told Finn I'd go through with the test. So, good or bad, I'm sticking to my word."

Rising from the couch, he joined her at the window. "I'm glad to hear you say that. Now, let's forget about the Calhouns for a moment. This morning you mentioned seeing Lake Tahoe. Would you like to go tomorrow, before I have to head back to work on Monday?"

"Back to work? I had the impression that you worked at your leisure—here from your house."

He chuckled and the rich, sexy sound warmed her as much as the heat from the fireplace. "I'm not that independent yet, Sassy. I work Monday through Friday out of an office on the Silver Horn."

"You have that much to keep you busy? Don't you just deal with wills and legal things like that?"

"I do. But that type of work only happens occasionally. Most of my duties consist of sales contracts dealing with cattle, horses and mineral rights. I have to go through each and every one of them to make sure there are no loopholes that might create future losses or problems for the ranch. One wrong word, like 'if,' 'and' or 'but,' could cost the Horn thousands."

"I see," she said thoughtfully. So that meant Jett would be gone for a big part of the day throughout the workweek. The idea should have filled her with relief. Instead, she was thinking how quiet the place would be without him around.

"So, what about Lake Tahoe? Are you game for the trip? It's only a few miles over to the eastern shoreline. We can see as much of it as you want, then drive up to Reno and have lunch."

Her heart was suddenly thumping at high speed. "This sounds like a date," she said guardedly.

Grinning, he moved closer, and Sassy found herself gazing up at his face, searching the strong, chiseled nuances of each feature, the dark stubble shadowing his jaw. She'd never been so fascinated by a man's face or so mesmerized by the memory of a kiss.

"Is anything wrong with that?" he asked.

The only thing wrong was her ridiculously happy reaction. Or should she think of it as wrong? She could spend special time with Jett without falling madly in love with him, she assured herself. She was stronger and smarter than to allow her emotions to take control of her.

"Nothing wrong. I'd very much like to go. But will the snow cause a problem on the highways?"

"The DOT usually keeps the major highways pushed clear. And the snow on the mountains would make for a pretty drive.

But I promise, if the roads look treacherous we'll wait. I don't want to put you or the little one in danger."

Such simple words, Sassy thought. But they felt like a ray of warm sun to her. "What time should I be ready?"

"No later than nine-thirty. That should give me and Noah enough time to finish the feeding chores. Is that okay with you?"

She smiled at him. "It's a date."

He smiled back at her. Then, all of a sudden, the smile disappeared and he turned his gaze to the window. Long, pensive moments ticked by in silence, eventually prompting Sassy to draw close enough to rest a hand on his forearm.

"Jett, is anything wrong?" she asked gently. "If you're thinking you'd rather withdraw the invitation, I'll understand."

"I don't want to withdraw anything I've said to you or done to you." He turned toward her, his expression solemn. "I was just thinking how long it's been since I've wanted to be with a woman. And now—here I am wanting to spend more and more time with you."

"You make it sound like you've come down with an illness or something."

He shook his head. "If you'd been through

what I have, you'd understand." He stared once again at the window and the falling snow. "You've probably already guessed that I've been married."

For some reason his revelation struck her hard. "No. But I've wondered."

He sighed. "I divorced Erica more than five years ago."

"How long were you married?"

"Three years," he muttered. "Long, turbulent years."

It didn't make sense, Sassy thought. His ex was gone and had been out of his life for several years, yet the mere thought of Jett loving another woman filled her with jealousy.

Swallowing, she searched for a reply that wouldn't sound hackneyed or offensive, but without knowing what had occurred with his marriage, it was impossible. "I'm sorry things didn't work out for you," she finally said.

"Don't be. The marriage should've never happened. We were all wrong for each other. And it was my fault for not realizing that before I married her."

Sassy hadn't expected him to share such a personal part of his life with her. And she'd been telling herself that the less she knew about the man, the easier it would be to keep her distance emotionally. But now that he was talking, her heart was crying out to know more.

"Was she from this area?"

"No. I met her while I was in college at UNLV. She was petite, dark-haired and very beautiful. I was smitten from the first moment I saw her. We dated about six months before we married. By then, I believed I knew everything I needed to know about her and my feelings toward her. But I was wrong. Now that I look back, I think I saw her faults all along, but I chose to ignore them and hope they'd go away." A fatalistic smile twisted his lips. "Don't get me wrong, Sassy. I had faults, too. Everybody does. Some are just more serious than others. And Erica's turned out to be the serious kind."

"Oh. Was she unfaithful?"

Turning away from the window, he walked over to the fireplace. As he used the poker to stoke the fire, he said, "Not at all. In fact, in her eyes I was the only man on earth."

Sassy moved over to the couch and resumed her earlier seat. "And that was bad?"

"Very bad, Sassy. I couldn't be away from her for two or three hours without her thinking I was with another woman or wanting to be with one. She was consumed with jealousy."

"Did she have reason to be?"

Standing on the hearth, he turned his back to the fire and cast a weary look at her. "No. My Lord, I'd married the woman I loved. Why would I immediately start looking for another one? I tried everything I could to make Erica see she had nothing to worry about, but the more I tried, the worse she got. I finally realized she was basically an insecure person, and that marriage was more than she could deal with. Her doubts and fears grew to the manic point."

"Do you know why she lacked self-confidence?"

"That's the mystery of it, Sassy. She was pretty, smart and well educated. She had loving parents and siblings, and a great job as a secretary for a city administrator. But that wasn't enough. For some reason her insecurities grew and grew, until she began clinging to me like a helpless child."

"How sad," Sassy murmured.

"Sad was just a part of it. The turmoil between us began to take a toll on her health. She developed all sorts of dependencies and I ended up being more of a prisoner than a husband. It became an unbearable situation. We'd married for better or worse, but the marriage wasn't helping her, either."

Sassy was stunned. Jett seemed like a sensible man and slow to anger. The fact that he endured such a nightmarish relationship for three long years told Sassy he must have loved his ex-wife very much. "So you finally put an end to it."

Returning to the couch, he eased down beside her and the bitterness she saw on his face told her that the pain of his failed marriage was still haunting him.

"We tried counseling but it didn't seem to help. And when she felt threatened by my talking to any woman—even to Bella—well, after that I didn't see much point in trying to hang on."

"If she was so obsessive over you, I can't imagine her letting go nicely. Does she still live around here?"

"Oddly enough, she was so mentally and physically drained by then that she didn't put up a fight over the divorce. She accepted it was over between us and moved back to Las Vegas. About a year later, I received a letter from her father telling me he'd managed to get her into therapy and that she'd finally recognized she had problems. He said he was sorry for everything his daughter had put me through." Pausing, Jett shook his head. "Sorry. As if that would take all the damage away."

"What else could he say?" Sassy asked softly. "The man understood that words couldn't fix the hurt. Deep down, I think you understand that, too."

"Yeah. It was too late to fix anything. And now—well, when you said I was a man who'd sworn off love—you were close to being right."

In spite of the heat radiating from the fireplace, Sassy felt a chill wash over her. It shouldn't matter to her whether this man was capable of loving anyone, much less her. Yet it did. Jett deserved to have more in his life. He deserved to be happy and have someone to share in that happiness.

"What do you mean, close to being right?"

His brown eyes were full of anguish as they connected with hers. "It means I'm not exactly sure how I feel about love. For a long time after my divorce, I even doubted such a thing existed. What Erica and I had certainly wasn't love."

"Surely you loved her when you married her?"

"I believed I did. But if love can crumble that quickly, then it's not something I want to invest in ever again."

His cynical statement was probably justified, but it rubbed every womanly cell inside of her the wrong way, and before she could catch herself, Sassy's jaw clamped tight. The words rolling off her tongue were just as stiff.

"You have a right to feel the way you do, Jett. But why tell me? Are you afraid I have designs on you or something and you feel the need to warn me off? If that's the case, then you've been wasting your time. Just because I called our outing tomorrow a date doesn't mean you need to go into panic mode. If you're that worried, go ahead and call the whole thing off."

"Sassy, that's not what—"

Horrified that she'd not kept a better rein on herself, she quickly jumped to her feet. "Sorry, Jett. I shouldn't have gone off on you like that—I'd better go to bed before I say any more."

She started to walk off, but Jett leaped off the couch and snatched a hold on her arm.

"Wait just a minute, Sassy. You're not going

to throw something like that at me and then walk off!"

She whirled around as hot color washed over her face. "Jett, I was out of line. Please, let's leave it at that."

"Sassy, I don't care if you speak your mind. I'm glad that you feel comfortable enough with me to do that. What I don't understand is why you're angry with me."

With a heavy sigh, she stared at her feet. "Jett, it was— It made me feel special for you to share that private glimpse of your marriage. But then you had to go and ruin it all with that last remark."

"Why did that ruin it? Because I busted your romantic bubble about love and marriage?"

That jerked her head up. "No! If you want to live like an unfeeling rock that's your business. But why tell me? I'm not weak-willed, and though I fainted the other day, I'm not ill. I didn't come here looking for love—or anything like it."

With his hand on her shoulder, he moved forward until the front of his body was pressed against hers. "Sassy, I think I should tell you that the warning was more for myself, not you."

His eyes were locked on hers and the heat of his body was arcing into hers like a wildfire leaping from one branch to the next. His chest was practically flattening her breasts while his hips reminded her he was all man. And she was melting like a snowflake on a warm cheek.

"Jett, this is crazy—"

"Sassy, Sassy. I don't want to love you. I only want to touch you. I want to hold you in my arms and feel your skin against mine, taste the sweetness of your lips."

As everything inside her began to tremble, she realized she couldn't deal with this or him. Her senses were too weak and willing for her to fight against the pleasures of being this close to him.

"It won't work, Jett. I won't go to bed with you. The next time I let a man touch me in that way, I'll have to be in love with him. And him with me."

Even as she spoke her vow, his head was lowering, his breath skimming across her face like a sweet whisper.

"I'm not asking you to go to bed with me. Not yet."

There wasn't even time for her to gasp before his lips came down on hers, and by then

Sassy was a willing prisoner to the tantalizing taste of his kiss. She didn't want to back away. And she especially didn't want to think about tomorrow. Being in his arms took her to a special place. One that she never wanted to leave.

Her lips parted and, as he deepened the kiss, his hands thrust into her hair and tilted her head to one side. Beneath her breast, her heart was hammering, and before she could stop them, her arms slid around his waist.

Sassy wasn't sure how long the kiss went on. She was too absorbed in Jett for her mind to register the passing of time. But eventually the sound of Bella entering the front door was enough to rip two of them apart.

Dazed, Sassy slapped a hand over her mouth. Then, darting a frantic look toward the entryway, she whirled and ran from the room.

The next morning dawned clear and the sun sparkled off the snow that blanketed the open mesa and decorated the distant mountain tops like white lace on green velvet. The change in the weather helped to lift Jett's spirits. Especially after he learned all the major highways were clear and it would be safe enough for him and Sassy to travel up to Reno.

But later that morning, as he readied himself for the outing, he wondered what the hell he was doing getting himself involved with Sassy. They were both saying one thing and doing exactly the opposite. She wanted love from a man. He could see it all over her face, hear it in her words. He couldn't give her that much of himself. He didn't want to give any woman that much of a hold over him again. And yet, it made him happy to be with her. After dealing with Erica's frailties, Sassy's proud determination to forge ahead and make a future for herself and her baby was especially endearing to him. Then there was the sound of her voice and the richness of her smile, which were just as bewitching as her fiery hair and blue, blue eyes.

Face it, Jett, you're tumbling head over heels for the woman. She's going to take your heart and wring it between her two little hands until there's nothing left inside it.

Fed up with the voice going off in his head, Jett finished buttoning his shirt and reached for the sheepskin jacket lying on the foot of the bed. For the first time in years, he felt excited about life. He wasn't going to let anything ruin that today. Even the thought of losing his heart.

Ten minutes later, Jett steered the truck beneath the entrance to the J Bar S and turned south on Highway 50. Across the seat from him, Sassy silently stared out the passenger window. She'd hardly said more than ten words to him since they'd started the trip, and he wondered if she was pouting over the cross words they'd exchanged last night, or their kiss, or if something else was on her mind. Like the baby or the Calhouns.

Damn, damn, Jett. The woman has enough on her plate without you trying to wedge your way onto it. So, why are you trying?

"Do you like the snow?"

Her simple question jarred his wandering thoughts and he took a moment to gather them before he spoke.

"I like the moisture it puts in the ground. God knows around here we never get enough of it. But since cattle can't graze through drifts of snow, it's hard on them. You already know about the snow and feeding cattle, though."

"Hmm. I should've guessed you'd look at it from a rancher's point of view. If I owned a ranch, I probably would, too."

He could feel her gaze traveling over the side of his face and it urged him to glance her way. The picture she made, sitting beside him, made the sky seem bluer, the sun even brighter and turned him into a complete sap.

"And how do you see the snow, Miss Sassy?"

"When it first falls it makes everything look new and fresh. Like the world is starting all over. That's what I like best about it."

"Is that what you'd like to do? Start all over?"

Silent moments passed before she finally said, "Not exactly. I've made mistakes. But that's how we learn, isn't it? And I don't want to look back with regret. I want to move forward to where everything is fresh and new."

Was that what he'd been doing? Jett wondered. Looking back with regrets instead of reaching for a better future? He didn't want to think he'd wasted these past five years just licking his wounds and trying to avoid being hurt all over again. But now he was wondering if that's exactly what he had been doing.

Reaching for a knob on the dash, he adjusted the heater so that part of the warm air would blow on her feet. "Last night, after you raced off to your room, I expected you'd cancel our trip this morning."

He glanced over just in time to see her features tighten.

"Thank God your sister chose that moment to enter the house," she muttered.

He had to grin. "Hmm. I was thinking Bella had very bad timing."

Sassy lifted her chin to a defiant angle and Jett realized he admired her pluckiness as much as her vibrant beauty. "Well, I'm not a coward, Jett. I wasn't about to let that kiss scare me away from you or this outing. You can kiss me all you'd like, but you're not going to break my resolve concerning you."

"Kiss you all I want, huh? That sounds like a pretty pleasurable challenge to me."

"That wasn't a challenge. That was a promise."

His chuckle was low and sexy. "Well, promises are made to be broken, Sassy. And resolves can be broken, too."

After traveling through Carson City, the eastern shoreline of Tahoe Lake was only a few short minutes away. Jett drove to one of the more easily accessible beaches and

stopped the truck in a paved parking area surrounded by huge ponderosa pines and red firs.

"There's a wooden dock not far from here
that goes out over the water. Do you feel up
to walking?" he asked.

She reached to unfasten her safety belt.
"Sure. I'd love to get a closer view."

"Great. Just wait until I help you down.
The ground is slick. I don't want you going
anywhere unless you're holding on to me."

She shot him an impish grin. "Okay, Jett.
I'll let you lead me around like an old granny
woman," she teased.

Moments later, he helped her to the ground
and she buttoned her coat and fastened a thick
green scarf around her neck before he led her
away from the truck.

"Cold?" he asked, as a breeze from the
north ruffled her red waves.

"No. The sun feels wonderful."

He took a careful hold on her arm, and they
started over a small trail that led downward
to the shoreline. Along the way, huge boul-
ders rose above their heads and wind whistled
through white firs and giant pines.

Other than the two of them, there was nothing around but the birds swooping over the

span of deep blue water that stretched as far as the eye could see.

"The water looks so clear," she remarked. "Just how big is this lake?"

"It's twelve miles wide and more than a thousand feet deep."

Clearly impressed, she said, "Oh, we don't have anything like this around Ruidoso."

"You won't find any other lake like this in North America. Guess that's why the tourists flock to it."

Using her cell phone, she snapped several pictures before turning a smile on him that said she was enjoying every moment. The idea that he'd managed to please her made him ridiculously happy.

"This is so gorgeous, Jett. And practically right here in your backyard. Do you come here often?"

"No. I really don't have a reason to drive over here. When Bella and I were just little kids, our parents would bring us here during the summer for swims and picnics. One thing about Dad, he liked to enjoy himself. He'd bring his guitar and make up silly little songs around the campfire." He smiled a bit. "Funny, even though our father would be gone for long stretches at a time, it was very special for us all whenever he was home. We adored him."

Resting her back against the railing on the dock, she looked up at him. "Was he kind to you?"

"I don't recall him ever raising his voice to me or Bella. But then he left most of the disciplining up to Mom. I never did have much in common with my dad. We had totally different interests. But sometimes I really miss him—just hearing him laugh—seeing his face."

"Would you like for him to come around?"

"Only if it was because he wanted to see his kids. Not because he was feeling guilty."

"Well, at least you have a father," she said with a small sigh.

"You do, too. Somewhere," he said. Then, in an effort to lift the somber moment, he smiled and touched a fingertip to the bridge of her nose. "Out here in the sunlight I can see your freckles."

"You shouldn't be looking at my freckles. Especially with all this beauty around us."

"Your freckles are very charming." To emphasize his point, he bent his head and kissed several spots along her cheekbone. As his lips hovered near her nose, he felt her fingers momentarily tighten over his forearm, then just as her flowery scent filled his head, she suddenly turned her back to him.

"We should be going."

Her voice was small and strained and he wondered if she wanted to be in his arms as much he wanted her to be there. "Sassy, before we go I—I'm glad you still wanted to come on this date with me."

Her head twisted around, and as she stared at him in wonder, strands of red hair blew across her face and clung to her moist lips. Jett's fingers itched to clear them away and press his mouth to all that sweetness.

"Is that what this really is, Jett?" she asked slowly.

A long breath rushed out of him. "I've been thinking about what you said last night. About me being an unfeeling rock, and I'm wondering if you might be right, Sassy. Maybe I don't know how to love. Maybe I'd like for you to teach me."

A wry sort of smile touched her lips, and then she reached for his hand and wrapped her fingers loosely around his. "Jett, what you feel for me is physical. I'll even admit that I have the same attraction to you. But we don't need to hash this out again. Let's just enjoy our time together today and the remainder of my days here in Nevada. Once I'm gone you'll be relieved you didn't get involved with a pregnant woman."

The fact that Sassy was pregnant didn't revolt him. It made him feel even more protective of her. It made him picture her with a child feeding at her breasts. His child.

What did it mean? That he was still capable of falling in love? That he was already seeing Sassy as his soul mate? Oh, God, he couldn't let that happen. No matter how much he enjoyed her company, no matter how much he wanted to take her into his arms and kiss her, and no matter that he desperately wanted her baby to have a daddy, he couldn't risk his heart again.

Urging her away from the edge of the dock, he said, "You're right. Let's go and enjoy the rest of the day."

Chapter 8

Monday morning, on the way to the Health Department in Carson City, Sassy tried not to think about the DNA test or what the results could possibly mean to her life. The sum of it was too overwhelming to consider. Besides, with Jett and the baby consuming her thoughts, there was hardly enough room for anything else.

Yesterday had turned out to be a fairy-tale trip for Sassy. After seeing the lake, they'd traveled up to Reno and eaten lunch in a hotel restaurant that overlooked an atrium filled with lush tropical plants and a waterfall. Afterward, they'd looked over part of the town, then headed through the old mining towns of Virginia City and Silver City before finally ending the big circle that started and ended on the J Bar S.

The sights had been a treat for Sassy, and the history interesting, but none of it had compared to having Jett's exclusive company. And though he'd not made any effort to kiss her again, the long hours she'd spent with him had somehow bonded her even closer to the man.

Maybe I don't know how to love. Maybe I'd like for you to teach me.

Oh, how his words had pierced deeply into her heart. And, at that moment, she'd wanted to wrap her arms around him. She'd longed to tell him to take her somewhere quiet and private, and make love to her all day long. But as much as she'd desired him, she'd tamped it down. Letting her heart lead her around by the nose wasn't going to take care of her and her baby's future.

"Are you nervous about this test, Sassy? You've hardly said two words since we left the ranch, and you're looking a bit peaked."

Jett wheeled the truck into a parking space near the Health Department building and killed the engine. Sassy reached to the floor-board for her handbag.

"I'm trying not to think about it," she said. She didn't go on to explain that she'd already lost her breakfast, and her stomach was still on a monster roller coaster. She didn't want him getting the notion that she needed to be coddled.

Glancing out the driver's window, he said, "Well, there's Finn driving up right now. Let's go get this over with."

Dressed in working cowboy gear, Finn met up with them on the sidewalk and, after a quick exchange of greetings, caught them up on Bart's condition.

"Grandfather's blood pressure is back to normal, so the doc plans to release him in a day or two. You can bet that Greta and Tessa aren't looking forward to his homecoming. He'll be giving them some hell. Not to mention barking plenty of orders at me and my brothers. But we're glad he's feeling better. The Horn isn't the same without the old man there."

"I'm very glad he's better," Sassy said, as the three of them migrated toward the entrance of the building.

"Amen to that," Jett added.

Inside the building, Finn went straight to the front desk and explained the reason for their visit. After that, she and Finn were required to fill out several forms and pay for the test. Something Finn insisted on doing with Calhoun funds.

With the facility already full of people, they sat through a lengthy wait. The time stretched Sassy's nerves and left her stomach feeling as if she were riding a wave instead of a solid chair. Just when she thought she might have to make an embarrassing dash to the bathroom, a nurse arrived to escort them to a small room. A male technician wasted no time in collecting their DNA, and after a few short minutes the three of them were outside the building and preparing to leave.

"Well, all that's left now is the waiting," Finn said cheerily.

"And how long is the normal wait for this type of test result?" Jett asked.

Since Jett had stayed behind in the lobby while the samples had been collected, Finn filled him in. "The tech said it all depends on how complex the test is and whether the lab is backed up on their work. The way he talked, we might get the results in anywhere from a week to a month."

A month sounded like an eon to Sassy. Especially since she'd put her job on hold to make this trip. Frankie had a heart condition. She didn't need to be overdoing it with household chores. And Leyla, who cooked for the family, had a four-year-old son and a newborn daughter. She didn't have time to tackle Sassy's job, too. Getting a temporary maid to fill in wouldn't be easy. The Chaparral was a remote ranch. It took thirty to forty minutes of traveling rough dirt road to get there.

Then, aside from her job, there was Jett. Living under the same roof with him for that length of time would definitely test her resolve to stay out of his bed. But she'd promised Finn and Jett that she would stick this out. She couldn't renege now.

"Hopefully it will turn out to be a week rather than a month," she remarked.

"And hopefully Bart will start talking before then," Jett added.

"Yeah," Finn said with a caustic laugh. "Miracles do happen. And that's just what it'll take to cure the old man of lockjaw."

Jett levered his hat down over his forehead and reached for Sassy's arm. "We'd better be going. I need to take Sassy home before I drive out to the Silver Horn."

"I can take her," Finn quickly offered. "I have enough time before I'm needed back at the ranch."

Not liking the idea that she was a nuisance for either man, Sassy interjected, "If one of you would take me to a car rental agency I can drive myself."

Jett arched a brow at her. "Car rental—"

Finn interrupted, "Hell, Jett, can't you give the woman something to drive? If you can't, we have plenty of vehicles she can borrow."

Frowning at Finn, Jett said, "This is the first I've heard about her wanting a car."

She wanted to scream at the both of them. Instead she tried to patiently explain. "I can hardly hang around here for an extended length of time without transportation. I'll rent a car and be done with it."

"By the time you pay that much rental cost you might as well have bought a vehicle. Forget it," Jett told her. "I have another truck you can use. Can you drive a truck?"

Before she could answer, her stomach took a sudden sickening lurch. Slapping a hand over her mouth, she raced down the sidewalk until she reached the nearest trash barrel.

She was still heaving, her head bent over

the edge of the bin, when she felt Jett's hand against her back.

"Sassy, do I need to take you to a doctor?"

Men. At the moment, her fascination with the male gender had gone into the trash heap. "No. I'm pregnant. Not sick."

"You are sick. You're vomiting."

Not daring to lift her head, she thrust her handbag back at him. "There's a tissue inside my bag. Would you please dig it out for me?"

He did as she asked, and after Sassy had carefully wiped her face and drawn in several long, cleansing breaths, she turned away from the trash bin to see both men staring tragically at her.

"Gosh, Sassy, you look awful," Finn stated with concern. "Are you that worked up about the test?"

Jett shot him a pointed look. "It's not the test. She's pregnant."

Finn's mouth formed a shocked O. "A baby?"

Sassy groaned. "You just had to tell him, didn't you?"

"I sure did," Jett answered. "He can see how sick you are. Besides, in a few weeks that tiny waist of yours is going to start bulging and everyone is going to be able to tell you're with child. You can't keep it a secret."

He was right. She wasn't ashamed of her pregnancy, she was thrilled about it, and now was as good as time as any to spread the news. "Sorry, Jett. I'm not trying to keep my condition a secret. But I don't want either of you feeling sorry for me. Once I get home and lie down I'll be perfectly fine."

"A baby," Finn repeated with a delighted grin. "Congratulations, Sassy! And just think. If it turns out that you are a part of the family, then there's another little Calhoun on the way!"

"I never realized you were such a family man, Finn," Jett said dryly.

"There's a lot you don't know about me, Jett." With a sly chuckle, Finn reached to pat Sassy on the shoulder. "Get her home. I'll call the business office and let them know you'll be a little late."

"Thanks, Finn. I'll catch up with you at the ranch."

The young rancher disappeared down the sidewalk, and Jett helped Sassy to the truck. Once she was settled in the seat, she leaned her head back and willed her stomach to stay put.

"Hellfire," Jett muttered as he backed the

truck onto the street and merged into the flow of traffic. "The way Finn was acting, anyone would think he was the expecting daddy."

Jett's snide remark had her glancing over at him. "He was happy for me, that's all. What's wrong with that?"

"Nothing. Nothing at all. I've just never seen him act so excited over someone having a baby."

"Could be he's never had the opportunity to get excited. He and his brothers don't have any children. You don't have any children. And whether I'm a Calhoun or not, I think Finn feels connected to me."

"I feel connected to you, too, Sassy."

She didn't ask him to explain what that comment meant, but she thought about it all the way home.

Later that morning, Jett was in his office, giving instructions to his secretary, Kim, a woman in her thirties with jet-black hair and gray eyes that she hid behind a pair of cat-framed glasses.

"I've highlighted all the sections to be edited. And be sure to remove the word 'jointly' here in the bottom paragraph. Also, I'm not certain these are the right numbers for the weight cost. Let me check those before you retype it."

She scooped up the stack of papers from his desk. "Of course, Mr. Sundell. I'll have this ready in just a few minutes."

As Kim hurried out of his office, Finn swaggered in and plopped into the leather chair positioned in front of Jett's desk.

"What's up?" Jett asked him.

Removing his hat, Finn used the brim to swat at the mud clinging to the bottom of his jeans. "Nothing. I just wanted to see how Sassy was doing."

"She was lying down when I left the ranch. She's visited the doctor and I think she'll soon get past this nausea stage." At least, Jett hoped so. Not only did it hurt him to see her suffering, it reminded him of all the ailments he'd tried to help Erica get through. By the end of their marriage her bad days had far outweighed the good ones, and he'd grown so weary of it, so tired of fetching and coddling. If she'd been really sick, that would have been one thing, but she'd used his protective nature to keep him close and at her bidding. Sassy welcomed him whenever he was around, but she didn't press him to stay close to her, and she encouraged him to go out and about. Even when they went to Tahoe, she was willing to wander off on her own and didn't get upset when he spoke to others around him. It was refreshing after Erica's neediness.

"I do, too." Finn slapped his hat back onto his head. "I—uh, told Dad about her being pregnant."

Linking his hands at the back of his neck, Jett leaned back in the plush leather desk chair. "Oh? How did he react?"

"He didn't say much. But a funny sort of look came over his face. I think he's worried, Jett."

"You'd look worried, too, if your father was being treated in the hospital."

"No. I think this is something about Sassy. When I told him about the baby, his whole demeanor suddenly changed. He got quiet and sorta preoccupied. Maybe you ought to talk to him about it, Jett. He might open up to you."

"Why me? Why not Clancy or Rafe or Evan?"

Finn frowned. "You're a lawyer. You just naturally know how to get people to talk."

Did he? Jett's grandmother, Adah, had always said that he pulled words out of people like a dentist pulled teeth. And because of her, he'd persevered through college and then law school. His grandmother had wanted him to be more than a man who raised cattle and horses. She'd wanted him to use his mind to make a living rather than his hands. But later, after he'd become a lawyer and taken on this high-paying job with the Calhouns, Adah had realized that she couldn't entirely take the cowboy out of her grandson. Now she and Jett's grandfather were proud of what he was building on the J Bar S.

"I won't put Orin on the witness stand. But I'll try to nudge him along," Jett said, finally.

Finn's expression suddenly turned rueful. "Like Sassy said, the DNA test will tell us the genetic information. But it's how and who that I want to know. To be honest, Jett, to think of my dad or grandfather siring another child outside their marriages does something to me. I didn't want to talk about it so bluntly in front of Sassy. But do you think that's what this is all about? Infidelity?"

"I don't know," Jett said honestly. "If that's what it turns out to be, would you regret finding out about Sassy?"

Rising to his feet, Finn shook his head. "No. Someone dropped Sassy on a doorstep like a puppy or a kitten. She deserves the truth of why someone treated her that way."

Yes, she deserved that, and so much more, Jett thought. She deserved to be truly loved. But could he ever be that man? And how would he react if she did grow ill from the pregnancy? Would he be able to face caring for another ill woman?

Later that afternoon, Jett walked to the outer part of his office and dropped a stack of legal papers onto his secretary's desk. "I've signed off on all of these, Kim. They're ready to go."

The young woman glanced up at him. "I'll send them right out, Mr. Sundell. Was there anything else you needed?"

"Not right now. I'm going to walk up to the big house for a while. If you need me for anything, I'll be there."

"Right. I'll hold any calls unless they're urgent," she told him.

Jett left the block of office buildings, and rather than drive the distance to the big ranch house, he walked up the long hill and entered through a side door.

Inside, a short hallway led him straight into the kitchen where Greta was pulling something wrapped in aluminum foil from the oven.

"Don't drop that!" Jett practically shouted. "I want a piece of it."

The older woman plopped the baking pan on the stove top before whirling in his direction. "Jett Sundell, I ought to take a broom to your backside! If I hadn't had such a good grip, the whole supper would have landed on the floor!"

Enjoying Greta's flustered reaction, he laughed. "And with Bart coming home, you would've been in deep trouble."

"Hah! The old man ain't getting any of this. Too much cholesterol for him. Instead of roast beef, he's getting a turkey patty."

"Greta, you must be deliberately plotting to run Bart's pressure up again just to get him out of the house."

The cook laughed and winked at him. "I'll save you some of the roast beef. You can take it home to your pretty redhead."

Jett opened his mouth to remind the cook that Sassy wasn't his redhead. But he liked the sound of it so much, he let it pass. "Thanks, Greta. I'll come back by the kitchen before I leave."

She shot him a clever grin. "Well, I hear she's eating for two, now. The food will do her good."

"Finn spreads news faster than the *Gazette*," Jett said with a shake of his head, then asked, "Do you know if Orin is in his study?"

"He should be. I just took him a fresh pot of coffee about five minutes ago."

"Thanks," Jett told her, then quickly left the kitchen and made his way to the back of the big house where Orin's study was located.

After a quick knock on the carved oak door, he stepped inside a large room paneled in dark wood and furnished with overstuffed navy blue chairs and a long matching couch. Orin was sitting behind a big cherry desk, a pen in one hand and a phone jammed to his ear.

The moment he spotted Jett, he silently motioned for him to come closer while quickly ending the conversation.

When Orin placed the receiver back on its hook, Jett said, "If that call was important you shouldn't have ended it for me. I can come back later."

"That call was to your office. You must have read my mind. I wanted to talk with you. Sit down and make yourself comfortable. Tessa just brought up coffee. I'll fetch us a cup."

"Thanks, I could use it," Jett told him.

While he took a seat in a straight-backed wooden chair positioned in front of Orin's desk, the other man walked over to a long table holding a tray with an insulated coffee pot and mugs, along with a silver sugar bowl and matching creamer.

"So, what's up?" Jett asked. "Are you considering purchasing some new holdings?"

"No. This is something more personal. That's why I didn't want to discuss it over the phone. And I'm glad you came now," Orin said as he filled two mugs with steaming coffee. "I have to leave in the next half hour to drive into town and pick up Dad. He's been throwing such a fit to come home, the doctor decided releasing him early would be better than him working himself into a boiling frenzy again. Dear God, that doctor deserves an award for dealing with a patient like Dad."

"I got a text from Finn a few minutes ago telling me about Bart coming home. You must be relieved."

Orin brought the coffee over to Jett, then sat down behind the desk with his own mug. "To some degree. But Dad's like a volcano. One never knows when he'll erupt."

Jett sipped the coffee. "So, if it's not business, what did you need to talk with me about?"

"Sassy."

Over the rim of his cup, Jett studied the other man closely. It wasn't surprising to hear that Orin had Sassy on his mind. Now that the DNA had been shipped off for testing, he figured the whole Calhoun family was thinking about her.

"Finn said he and his brothers talked with you about the DNA test they took this morning. But that you all decided to keep the information from Bart—for now, at least."

"That's right. We discussed it at length."

"And?"

Orin shrugged and, not for the first time, Jett noticed that the elder Calhoun was still a very fit and handsome man at the age of sixty-one. It made him wonder why Orin had mostly shut himself away in this house, or why he'd not remarried or shown any interest in women since Claudia had died. But then, Jett hadn't shown any interest in women, either. Until Sassy had come to town. Now he was more than interested—he was growing besotted.

"Whatever my sons want is what I want, too. Dad will just have to accept our wishes."

Jett let out a relieved breath. "I'm glad to hear that. Because, frankly, Finn believes his grandfather is hiding information regarding Sassy. Do you believe Bart is holding back?"

"Yes, I do believe it," Orin answered candidly. "But what the hell am I going to do about it, Jett? The man is too sick for me to take a run at him, demanding the truth. That's why I wanted to have a word with you before I bring Dad home tonight. Pressing him right now is out of the question. So, the way I see it, that leaves me and you digging elsewhere for as much information as we can find. Dad always was a stickler for keeping records. If we can find anything that might pertain to Sassy, then we'll wait for the right time to present it to him. He won't be able to avoid the truth then. What do you think?"

Jett thought the whole thing was pretty odd and that Bella was probably right. They were going to open a Pandora's box. But this was Sassy's life they were dealing with. He wanted the best for her, even if the truth splintered the Calhouns. Before meeting Sassy he could've never imagined feeling that way. Not when the Calhouns were like family to him. But now her happiness meant even more than that. How had that happened?

Unable to answer the question in his head, Jett asked the other man, "Where are these records stored? I hope somewhere away from Bart's eagle eye. If he sees us digging through old documents, he's likely to get suspicious."

"That won't be a problem. Most of the stuff is right here in my study." Orin pointed to a wide door just behind his left shoulder. "The storage room in there is filled with cabinets and a combination safe. Dad doesn't come in here all that much, and even if he catches us pilfering, we can make up some story that you needed old information for a contract or tax purposes or something."

Jett had to smile. "Now I see where Evan got his detective instincts."

Orin chuckled. "Not hardly, Jett. I'm just trying to solve a problem or a mystery. I'm not sure which one to call it."

Sassy might be upsetting Jett's peace of mind, and she was definitely creating havoc with his libido, but he couldn't think of her as a problem. "I'd call it a mystery, Orin."

"Well, let's hope we can solve it with whatever we can find in there." Using his head, he motioned toward the storage room behind him.

"What exactly is in there?" Jett asked.

"Birth, death and wedding certificates, along with insurance policies and wills. Those are the most important. The rest is older things that haven't been touched in years, like receipts pertaining to household purchases and personal expenses. But there might be something to give us some clues. It's worth a try, at least."

Sipping his coffee, Jett studied his old friend. Orin seemed open and sincere. Clearly, he wasn't expecting anything illicit to be exposed concerning himself. "I'm glad you suggested this, Orin. Because, like Sassy said, the DNA will only explain genetics. Not the who or why of it."

Pinching the bridge of his nose, Orin sighed. "Honestly, Jett, this whole thing has kept me up nights. Ever since Finn showed me that picture of Sassy I've felt something deep in my gut. And then when you brought her here and I saw her in person—I was jolted."

"So was Bart."

Rising from his desk, Orin left his coffee and began to pace back and forth in front of a picture window that framed a view of the Silver Horn ranch yard. The Calhouns owned a cattle empire, along with more assets that most regular folks could comprehend. But their riches hadn't necessarily kept heartache and loss from the family.

"Everyone knows Bart can be a real bastard at times. But he loved my mother so utterly. I can't imagine him cheating on her. But what other explanation is there? Where else could Sassy have come from?"

Hearing the anguish in Orin's voice, Jett couldn't help but feel for him. To think of his own father being an adulterer was far worse to Jett than Gary being a wayfaring ne'er-do-well. Apparently Orin held the same sentiments about Bart. But was that only anguish that Jett was hearing in Orin's voice? Perhaps part of it was something else, like guilt? Or regret? If he only knew.

"Orin, you're jumping the gun. The tests results could say there's no connection at all. Or there could be some other explanation. Maybe she's a child or grandchild from before marriage."

"Dad married Mom when they were both very young. Sassy would have to be a grandchild to fit that explanation. And you and I both know that's highly unlikely." He stopped his pacing long enough to look at Jett. "Finn tells me that Sassy is pregnant. He's all excited about it. I tell you, Jett, if Sassy isn't a part of the family, that boy is going to be crushed. For some reason I don't understand, he's become instantly attached to her."

What could he say? Jett asked himself. He'd become instantly attached to Sassy, too. And he couldn't understand why. "I don't think you need to worry about Finn. He's a practical guy."

Returning to his desk, Orin picked up his coffee mug. "I'm sure you feel like you've been wedged between two rocks. If having Sassy stay with you is causing any sort of problems, she's welcome to come here to the ranch."

For some reason, Orin's suggestion caused Jett to inwardly bristle. "Damn, Orin. That would hardly help Bart's blood pressure."

"This house is big enough that she could avoid him. Besides, I'm not going to coddle Dad. Part of his problem is that he's had his way too much."

"Well, I like having Sassy at the J Bar S," Jett said honestly. "And Bella's enjoying her company. So she's staying put."

One of Orin's dark brows lifted faintly. "Okay. Just thought I'd check. Since you and Erica divorced, you haven't exactly been, well, receptive to the opposite sex."

Jett couldn't remember the last time Orin or any of the Calhouns had mentioned his ex-wife. It was strange how Sassy's arrival had them all pondering the past and wondering about the future.

"Since Claudia died, I could say the same of you."

The older man sighed. "It still hurts too much, Jett. But that's something you understand, isn't it?"

"Yeah. I understand." Glancing at his watch, Jett rose to his feet and returned his mug to the coffee table. "I'd better go, Orin. I have some work to wrap up before I head home. And you need to leave for town."

Orin nodded. "Fine. Let's start on our search tomorrow."

"I'll be here."

Jett left the study and, before making his way out, dropped by the kitchen. As the cook had promised, she had a hefty container of the roast beef and accompanying vegetables dished up and ready for him to take home.

"This is kind of you, Greta. I hope Sassy is feeling well enough to eat."

The cook placed the container in a cardboard box, then handed the whole thing to him. "I hope so, too. Maybe my cooking will tempt her." She squinted up at him. "Uh…has Orin let anything slip about the girl?"

He frowned with confusion. "You mean regarding Sassy?"

Greta was clearly impatient. "Yes, I mean Sassy! What other girl has been around here?"

There was Tessa, the maid and five women working down at the business offices, but Jett didn't bother pointing that out. He expected Sassy had been the latest gossip all over the ranch, and Greta apparently expected Jett to understand that.

"What could Orin possible let slip?" Jett asked. "You told me and Sassy that Bart was the one who might know something."

Greta glanced over her shoulder to make sure the room was empty before she leaned closer and lowered her voice. "Bart is like a locked diary with all sorts of secrets. And I figure he has a few on Orin."

"Greta, you're making some wild accusations. Especially when there's not one man in this county who'd speak badly of Orin. And that includes me. I've never known of him to lie or cheat."

"I'm not accusing him of being a bad person, Jett. But he's human. For a while after little Darci died things were like a Deepfreeze around here. Claudia shut herself off from everybody." She leveled a pointed look at Jett. "When a man is shut out, you don't know where he might turn. That's all I'm saying."

Greta's gossip sounded reasonable. But that's all it was—gossip. "Greta, that's all hearsay. And Orin doesn't seem worried about finding anything out—he's helping us find out the truth."

Seeing he wasn't taking her information to heart, Greta shrugged both shoulders. "We're not dealing with the law here. Just regular folks. But you go ahead and think what you want. I'm just trying to help."

Frowning, he asked, "Greta, do you have any concrete proof that either Bart or Orin had an affair?"

She didn't hesitate to answer. "No."

"Twenty-four years ago, do you recall seeing a pregnant woman around here?" he persisted. "Any pregnant woman?"

She thought long and hard before she said, "That's a long time ago to remember something like that. But, no. I don't recall any pregnant women around here. Except for Claudia when she and Orin had their last one, Bowie. But he's twenty-three—that would've been later. And it's dang sure Claudia didn't give birth to Sassy. The woman rarely left this ranch for more than a day's time."

"I rest my case, Greta."

With the box of food cradled in the crook of one arm, he started out the door, while behind him Greta snorted loudly.

"Hmph! You ain't going to rest anything until you get to the bottom of this puzzle."

Greta was right about that, Jett thought a few moments later, as he walked back down the hill to his office. He wasn't going to rest until he found the truth. But what was that truth going to do to Sassy? Would it take her away from him?

He wasn't ready to say goodbye to Sassy yet. He wasn't sure he'd ever be ready to say goodbye to her. Did that mean he was ready to love again?

The question put a bitter taste on his tongue. He wasn't sure he'd ever felt that emotion or if he ever could. The only thing he was certain about was that he was feeling something for Sassy, and that "something" wasn't nearly as simple as old-fashioned lust.

Chapter 9

A week after that humiliating incident on the sidewalk in front of the Health Department, Sassy was still suffering from bouts of severe nausea that kept her mostly confined to bed. Four days ago, she'd given in to Jett's suggestion and allowed him to make an appointment for her with a local obstetrician, and yesterday he'd accompanied her to the doctor's office for the health visit.

Since she wasn't certain about the length of her stay here in Nevada, she'd been reluctant to start prenatal care with one doctor, then have to change in midstream when she returned to New Mexico. But the young doctor had assured her that she'd done the smart thing by coming to him. After a long, thorough exam, he'd pronounced her and the baby physically fit and prescribed a safe medication to help her get through the bouts of nausea. So far it was helping, but she was still weak and a bit queasy, so Jett was insisting she remain in bed until the medication took full effect. Sassy felt awful about the inconvenience she was causing, especially since Jett had been trying to do his legal work out of the house so that he could remain close and take care of her. Not being in his office on the Silver Horn was causing him extra work, but he wouldn't hear of leaving her alone.

Now she wondered what he was thinking. Was he getting tired of being tied to a sick woman? He'd mentioned before that his ex-wife had been the fragile and needy sort, and the issue of her mental and physical state had caused their marriage to deteriorate. Had Sassy's illness already caused him to lose his desire for her? Perhaps seeing her pale and miserable had made him have second thoughts? These past few days he'd been very caring, but distant somehow, and that troubled her greatly.

A slight rap on the door had her turning

her gaze away from the window to see Jett entering the room carrying a tray. This evening, he looked weary, and that made her feel even more guilty.

"I didn't realize it was already time for dinner," she said.

Easing down on the side of the bed, he placed the tray on the nightstand, then reached to help her prop the pillows behind her back.

He smiled faintly. "That's nice of you to call a cold sandwich 'dinner.'"

"The doctor said cold sandwiches were better for a queasy stomach than something hot. And I have to agree they seem to settle in my stomach better."

"Do you feel like eating this evening?"

"Actually, I do. I'm feeling much better. I even think I'll be able to be up and about tomorrow. So you'll be free to go on to the Silver Horn and work out of your office," she said happily.

"We'll see. I don't want you to rush."

She curled her fingers over his forearm. "I've already upset your work schedule too much. I'll be fine. I promise."

His gaze carefully scanned her face. "Let

me worry about my schedule, Sassy. I want you and the baby to be well."

Her eyes suddenly glowing, she squeezed his arm. "The baby is fine, Jett. Earlier today I thought I felt it move. It's probably too early in my pregnancy for that, but the fluttery feeling reassured me anyway."

"Sassy," he said softly, then reached over and placed a protective hand over her lower belly. "I'm sorry the pregnancy has made you so sick."

She dismissed his words with a wave of her hand. "Shoot, Jett, if a girl can't take a bit of nausea, then she's pretty wimpy. I'm already getting over this little hiccup and I've got my eyes on the prize."

A slow smile spread across his face. "You're incredible.

She said, "I hope you mean that in a good way."

"In a very good way." He pulled his hand away from her belly. "I've been wondering about something, Sassy. You've already told me that you don't have any family, but what about Barry's? Have you told them about the baby?"

She wondered if the lawyer in him was asking, or if he was simply interested as a man. "Barry's family split up years ago when his parents divorced. The only one he was close to was his father, Douglas. I plan to contact him when it's time for the baby to arrive."

His expression turned thoughtful. "That's good. The baby will have one grandfather, at least."

Sensing something else was on his mind, she asked, "Jett, are you— Have you heard something about the DNA test?"

Shaking his head, he picked up the tray of food and placed it across her lap. "No. Don't think about the test right now. Just eat and get well. That's all that really matters."

Much to Sassy's relief, the next morning she was feeling like her old self and was able to eat breakfast with Bella and Jett. She also managed to convince him to go to his office on the Silver Horn, and later that morning, when she was finally alone in the house, she called the Chaparral and gave Frankie the news about the coming baby. After the woman got past the initial shock, Frankie seemed very happy for Sassy and reminded her several times that the Cantrells would always be there to help and support her in any way they could. Sassy didn't hint at when she might be returning to New Mexico and her old job, and surprisingly, Frankie didn't prod her about it. Perhaps the other woman could sense that Sassy's life was taking a new and different turn, and they all needed to wait and see what the DNA test revealed.

For the remainder of the day, she texted some friends and caught up on news as she tried not to think about the DNA test or that Orin and Jett were searching through old family records, something he'd told her about this morning before he'd left for work. Compared to her feelings for Jett, learning her family identity was secondary now. She wasn't exactly sure when she'd come to that conclusion or what she should even do about it. Jett's heart wasn't ready for love or marriage. And she wasn't going to settle for less.

By the next afternoon, Sassy felt so good she was imbued with energy, and the need to get out and breathe fresh air had her donning a coat and leaving the house she'd been cooped up in for too many days. She and the two collies were walking along a cattle trail just north and west of the ranch house, soaking in the sunshine and sage-scented air when the sound of a vehicle caught Sassy's attention.

Shading her eyes with one hand, she looked up to see Jett's old work truck barreling toward her. A pair of startled sage grouse scattered out of its path, while a cloud of dust followed in its wake.

The man was certainly in a hurry, she decided, as she and the dogs stopped on the trail and waited for him to pull alongside her.

Before the driver's window was more than halfway down, he called out to her. "Sassy, what are you doing way out here?"

She strode up to the truck door. "Hello to you, too."

He blew out a breath of relief. "You had me worried. I was on the verge of calling Evan to tell him that the sheriff's department needed to start a search for you!"

Sassy rolled her eyes. "Honestly, Jett. I can almost see the ranch house from here. Besides, Mary and Max certainly know their way back home. Were you really worried that I was lost or something?"

Lifting the battered gray hat from his head, he thrust a hand through his hair, and Sassy could see he was struggling to collect himself.

"You didn't leave a note. I had no idea if you'd left with someone or walked away from the house and collapsed! You're just now starting to feel normal again."

Seeing the genuine worry on his face, she said, "I'm sorry I worried you, Jett. You and Bella never get home this early. I didn't write a note because I thought I'd be back to the house long before you arrived."

He shook his head. "Okay. No harm done. Climb in and I'll give you a ride."

She lowered the tailgate on the truck to allow the dogs to jump in before she climbed into the passenger seat and strapped herself in. As soon as she was settled, he pointed the truck toward home.

"I didn't see you at breakfast. I figured you were still sick," he said.

She smiled with happy relief. "Actually, I didn't miss breakfast because I was sick. For the first morning in days I didn't wake up nauseated. I was sound asleep. This afternoon I felt so good I couldn't stay cooped up in the house."

His lips twitched, but whether it was with a smile or frown, the movement was too faint to discern. Either way, it didn't matter. Just having the chance to drink in his masculine profile was pure delight.

"The day you made the feeding rounds

with me, I could tell you were enjoying being outdoors. When you talked about learning about ranching, though, I never imagined you literally hiked through cow pastures."

She laughed softly. "Hike or ride a horse. I do both. On the Chaparral there're lots of mountain trails on the ranch and sometimes Frankie rides with me. She's an excellent horsewoman. I'm just a novice, but I am learning to handle a horse pretty well. And in the summer I always make a vegetable garden and donate most of the produce to the needy. Leyla, Frankie's cook, is a good friend and we work the garden together. Plus, I like to grow flowers. All kinds of flowers. Oh, and I play on a summer-league softball team, too. And I like to fish and camp. What about you?"

Chuckling, he shook his head. "I'm out of breath just listening to all that."

"Seriously, Jett, I'm not sure you do anything for fun. Other than the day we went to Reno, all I've ever seen you do is work. Don't you have a hobby? Or things you like to do just for amusement?"

"Ranching is fun to me."

"That's good to hear. Otherwise I don't think you'd have any fun at all."

He darted a glance at her. "That's important to you, isn't it? Having fun?"

There was a note of disapproval in his voice, as though he considered doing enjoyable things a frivolous waste of time. His attitude irked her, but she tried not to let it show. "If you can't find a bit of fun in life, then what's the point, Jett?"

"Hmm. I probably seem like an old stuffed shirt to you. And perhaps I am. But a person changes after—"

When he didn't finish, she said, "After he gets knocked down. Yes, I know the feeling very well, Jett. But I don't plan to let anything keep me down."

"That's easier said than done, Sassy."

"There's nothing easy about it. In fact, it's really hard. That's what it is. But you and I are cut from different cloth, Jett. I was raised poor, and though I'd like to further my education, I've not had a chance to do it yet. I've never owned much of anything, so I hardly have to worry about losing my assets. But I don't have to party to enjoy myself. I find fun in simple things—like riding a horse or watching my zinnias grow. You say your fun is ranching, but is that because you love doing it, or because you love the money it puts in your bank account?"

He braked the truck to a stop near the barn door and turned an annoyed look on her. "Do you realize how insulting that long-winded speech was to me?"

"It wasn't meant to pacify you," she said bluntly, then quickly climbed out of the truck and headed toward the house.

After letting the dogs out of the truck bed, Jett followed close on her heels, but said nothing until they entered the house and the scent of cooking food met them at the kitchen door.

"What's that I smell?"

"Supper. It should be done in about thirty minutes."

Removing her coat, she hung the garment on the hall tree standing near the door, then used her hands to tame the wisps of hair that had loosened from her ponytail.

"You can cook? I mean more than frying an egg or making toast?"

Laughing at his amazed reaction, she turned to see he'd walked over to the oven and was peeking inside at the bubbling enchilada casserole.

"Sure I can," she answered as she walked

over to the sink to rinse her hands. "I am a woman."

He walked over to where she stood, and Sassy was instantly reminded that it had been several days since he'd touched her in an intimate way. And now she longed to lay her hands upon his chest, to lift her mouth up to his.

She'd sworn to him that she wouldn't succumb to his kisses. That she wouldn't have sex with him unless love was his motive. But what about her own motives? Was she beginning to love this man?

He said, "Being a woman doesn't automatically make you a cook. Erica struggled to heat a can of soup."

Shrugging, she fought to rein in the erotic thoughts zipping through her head. "I've lived alone for a long time. Necessity forced me to learn how to cook. And this evening, because I'm feeling so much better, I wanted to give you and Bella a break from fixing dinner."

A soft light warmed his brown eyes while a sheepish smile crossed his face. "I'm sorry if I sounded cross earlier," he said gently. "I was worried, that's all."

Her heart was suddenly pounding, yearning to touch him. "And I'm sorry that I worried you."

Lifting a hand, he smoothed fingertips along her cheekbone. "The color is back in your face. That makes me happy, Sassy."

"Thank you for taking care of me," she whispered.

He didn't say anything, and as she gazed back at him she could feel electricity building between them, threatening to spark at the slightest movement.

"Sassy—"

Before he could say more, the cell phone attached to his belt rang. With a heavy sigh, he turned away and answered the call. "What's wrong?" he asked the person on the other end of the connection. "Are you having car trouble or something?"

There was a long pause and then he said, "Oh. I see. So how long will you be down there? And what about clothes and things?"

Another pause, and then he said, "All right. Stay in touch. We'll see you when you get back."

He ended the call and turned back to Sassy. "That was Bella. She won't be coming home this evening. She and her boss are leaving for Las Vegas in about an hour. They'll be down there for a few days. Maybe a week. Something to do with a case he's been handling."

That meant she and Jett would be alone in the house. Together. The mere thought made her tremble with a mixture of alarm and excitement.

"I didn't see her leave with any bags this morning. Won't she need her clothes and things to take with her?"

"She said she had enough things stored there at the office to get by with. And, knowing Bella, she'll use the trip as an excuse for shopping."

"Oh. Well. Looks like we won't be seeing her for a while." Knowing there was probably a telling look on her face, she quickly stepped around him and hurried over to the oven.

As she peeked in at the casserole, Jett walked up behind her.

"Sassy, you don't have to run from me."

Nervously licking her lips, she closed the oven door and turned to face him. "I'm not running or leaving for a hotel in town."

For long, taut moments his gaze swept over her face, then finally he said, "Good. How long until we eat? I'd like to shower and change."

"Twenty minutes. I'll have everything on the table by then."

By the time Jett returned to the kitchen, Sassy had prepared a tossed salad, along with a basket of tortilla chips to go with the casserole. After adding two glasses of iced tea to the cozy table, he helped her into her seat then took his place across from her.

"It's good to see you eating real food again."

"I'm starving. I even made a pie. I found a can of cherries in the pantry. I hope you weren't saving them for something special."

He looked across at her and smiled. "This meal is something special."

It was certainly special to her. For the past week she'd not felt well enough to really enjoy his company. Now she was going to have him all to herself. "Maybe you'd better reserve that comment until after you eat," she said jokingly.

After they'd both filled their plates and began to eat, Jett said, "Bart caught me and Orin going through some of the old files this afternoon."

Her fork paused in midair. "Oh. What happened? What did you tell him?"

"Orin told him we were hunting some old

income tax files. That we needed some past numbers to compare with recent profit figures."

"Did he believe you?"

"I doubt it. He didn't look convinced. He just turned on his heel and left the study."

Sassy shook her head ruefully. "Jett, is it really necessary for you and Orin to do all this searching? I don't want Bart to get sick again. And the DNA will eventually tell us if I'm a Calhoun."

"Yes. But, like you said, it won't tell you who gave birth to you. Or why you were left on the orphanage's doorstep," he reminded her. "And Orin isn't stopping with searching the files. He's been calling old acquaintances and asking if they remember any baby rumors connected with Bart or anyone in the family twenty-four years ago."

"Have either of you found anything?"

"We're not sure."

Surprise once again stopped her fork before it reached her mouth. "You mean you might have found something? What?"

He reached for his tea glass. "Two canceled checks written by Bart about six months before you were born. Unfortunately, there wasn't a specific name in the recipient line—

they were made out to 'Cash.' One check was for five thousand dollars, the other for ten thousand. And no reason was listed on the 'For' line."

She ate a forkful of salad before she commented. "Jett, I don't see anything suspicious about that. People write checks solely for cash all the time. Especially before debit cards came into use."

"That's true. And even back then fifteen thousand would've been peanuts to the Calhouns. But there is no sign of the withdrawals listed in the ledger book. Orin tells me that back during that time Claudia did all the family bookkeeping, but once Darci became ill and passed away, she quit and Bart took over the job."

"But that doesn't make sense, Jett. If Bart didn't want anyone knowing about the withdrawals, he would have destroyed the canceled checks. Wouldn't he?"

"Orin and I have been batting that theory around, too. And our thinking is that by the time the canceled checks came in a month later, he simply forgot to do away with them."

Sassy shook her head. "Okay. Even if he was hiding something, it doesn't mean it pertained to me."

"You're exactly right. But the checks do have us wondering. Orin doesn't want to question his father yet. But later on I expect him to."

She'd already swallowed a bite of food, yet her throat felt thick and tight. She looked down at her plate as she tried to clear away the uncomfortable feeling.

"What's the matter, Sassy? Is the food up-setting your stomach?"

Looking up, she did her best to smile at him, but her effort only produced a weak semblance of one. "No. It just—well, every-thing you're saying—that would mean Bart paid off someone to keep me out of the fam-ily. Isn't that the way you see it?"

Understanding filled his eyes as he reached across the table to touch his fingers to hers. "I'd say we could stop this whole thing and forget it, Sassy. But it's gone too far to stop now. And you've always recognized the fact that someone gave you away. It's not like you believed you came from a pair of perfect par-ents."

Shaking away that glum thought, she lifted her chin. "I can take the truth, Jett. It might not be easy. But, like I told you earlier, I'm not going to let anything get me down. Not even Bart Calhoun."

He smiled. "Good girl. Now, eat your supper. I don't want those roses in your cheeks to fade."

A half hour later, after finishing pie and coffee, Sassy rose to her feet to clear away the table.

Standing up, Jett said, "You did the cooking. I'll do the cleaning up."

"It feels great to be up and doing, Jett. I'll have this done in no time. But if you insist on helping then I won't argue."

Jett gathered up a few of the dirty dishes and was following her over to the cabinets when a knock sounded on the door.

"Now, who could that be?" he wondered out loud.

Leaving the armload of dishes on the end of the bar, he went to the door.

"Hey, Noah, come in," he said warmly. "I'm glad you stopped by. I want you to meet Sassy. And we just finished eating. You can have the leftovers."

Sassy looked around to see a big man near Jett's age stepping into the house. A chocolate-brown hat covered longish black hair and shaded part of his dark features. A tan ranch coat covered broad shoulders, and the spurs on his boots jangled as he moved farther into the room.

Curious, she walked over to where the two men stood.

"Sassy, this is Noah Crawford, my friend first and my hired hand second," Jett introduced. "And this is Sassy Matthews, Noah, the woman from New Mexico I told you about."

Sassy extended her hand to the big man. "Nice to meet you, Noah. I'll get you a plate. I hope you like enchiladas and cherry pie."

"Sounds good, ma'am, but I'm in a hurry." He turned a serious look on Jett. "Sorry to interrupt, Jett, but I found a cow down in the second wash near that band of Joshua trees. I need some help with her."

Even before the other man had finished talking, Jett was pulling on his coat and hat. "Calving?"

Noah nodded, and Jett said, "I figured we had at least two, maybe three more weeks before that started."

"Mother Nature moves whenever she wants," Noah replied.

Sassy looked eagerly to Jett. "If you don't mind, I'd like to come along."

Clearly her request had caught him off guard. "It might not be a pretty sight, Sassy," he hedged.

She grabbed her coat from the hall tree and began pulling it over her jeans and sweater. "I've seen tough births before," she assured him. "I might even be able to help."

He hesitated, but then seemed to understand that she needed to join in. "All right. Let's get going," he said.

Several minutes later, the work truck came to a halt at the bottom of a narrow gulch still muddy from the snowmelt of a few days before. A few yards beyond the vehicle, the distressed cow lay near the twisted trunk of an ancient juniper tree, and Sassy's eyes misted over at the sight of her.

"Do you have any idea how long she's been here?" Jett questioned the other man as the three of them made their way over to the distressed animal.

Noah answered, "This morning, when I fed her, she was with the rest of the herd. After that it would be hard to say. I left this area to go patch fence."

"Well, let's hope we can help her without having to call out a vet," Jett said.

Once they reached the cow it was obvious

the birthing process had begun, but the calf had stuck in an awkward position.

Careful to position herself behind the cow's head, just in case the animal decided to jump to her feet and lunge forward, Sassy knelt by the Hereford and stroked her between the ears and down the side of her neck. Behind her, the two men began to pull on the calf with all their strength.

She whispered to the cow, "It'll be okay, girl. Just relax and let them help you."

After about five minutes with no results, both men were heaving for air.

"This isn't working, Jett. She needs a C-section."

"Too late for that, man. We'll have to get this calf out ourselves. I'll get the puller from the truck."

Sassy jumped to her feet. "I'll get it."

She raced off to the truck, and as she lifted the device from the bed of the truck, she prayed that the men wouldn't have to use it. And her prayer must have been answered immediately, because as she hurried over to the men with the birthing tool, she heard Jett's strained voice saying, "It's coming now, Noah! One more heave and I think we'll have it!"

She was thankful Jett's prediction was correct, and Sassy let out a cry of sheer relief as a little red calf slid clear of its mother.

"Thank God, you won't have to use this now!" She tossed down the puller and moved in for a closer view of the calf. "Is the little fella going to be okay?"

"Don't know yet, ma'am," Noah answered.

Jett quickly untied the bandana around his neck and used the green square of fabric to clean the calf's nose of birth debris and mucus.

"It's not breathing," Jett said bleakly. He opened the baby's mouth and cleared away more mucus, yet the calf continued to lie motionless.

Sassy elbowed her way between the two men. "Let me try."

Before either of them could guess her intentions she knelt over the calf and positioned her hands just behind its shoulder. In a firm, up-and-down motion she began to pump the calf's side, and after several long moments, the baby began to splutter and mew with signs of life.

Noah said in an awed voice, "Would you look at that!"

"I am looking," Jett replied.

Whooping with joy, Sassy leaped to her feet and flung her arms around Jett. He hugged her close for a brief moment, then purposely set her at arm's length.

"Where did you learn how to do that? I've never seen it done. Have you Noah?"

"Nope. I've seen old ranchers blow in a calf's mouth, and I've watched them hold a calf up by its heels and shake it. But not this."

Feeling happy and proud of herself, Sassy let out a breathless laugh. "Well, I learned it from a girlfriend back on the ranch. She's an assistant to the resident vet there. Well, actually, Lauren is his wife. And she's worked with him for so many years that she's almost a vet herself. Anyway, I've seen her do this more than once."

Jett's head swung back and forth with amazement. "You told me you were learning about ranching during your off time on the Chaparral, but I had no idea you'd learned this much!" Jett exclaimed.

The proud smile on her face belied her indifferent shrug. "I especially like helping Lauren with the sick and injured animals—learning how to care for them."

Noah said, "Hey, Jett, did you hear that

part about the resident vet? Must be a fancy place."

"I wouldn't call it fancy," Sassy declared. "The Chaparral has everything a ranch needs. The house is big but it's not lavish or anything. And the Cantrells are great folks. You'd never guess they're worth millions. They even own a gold mine."

"I'd say your job is secure," Noah said with a chuckle.

She glanced over at Jett and noticed an odd look had come over his face, but before she could figure what that was all about, he stepped around her and said to Noah, "We'd better see how the cow is faring."

The three of them waited until both mother and calf were on their feet and the baby had enjoyed its first meal before they climbed into the truck and headed back to the ranch. By then, nearly two hours had passed. Darkness had settled in, and without the sun, the temperature was rapidly dropping.

When they arrived at the ranch yard, Sassy left the two men to finish the last of the chores around the barn and walked on to the house. Inside, she went to work putting away the leftover food and placing all the dishes in the dishwasher.

After she'd fed Walter a can of salmon, then wiped down the table and countertops, she went to the bedroom to change out of her clothes. Mud and stains from handling the newborn calf were smeared down the front of her jeans and along the hem of her sweater. As she tossed them into a wicker hamper, she doubted either garment would come out of the wash spot free, but that hardly mattered. Mother and baby were going to be fine, and that made Sassy feel very good.

Mother and baby. The connotation of those two words caused her to pause and walk over to the dresser mirror. With only a lacy bra and panties covering her intimate parts, she turned sideways and carefully studied her image.

These past few days she'd been noticing the subtle changes in her body. The extra fullness to her breasts, the faint bulge at the lower part of her belly. Touching her fingers to the slight bump, a sudden rush of love overwhelmed her and brought a mist of tears to her eyes. Her own little baby was growing there, and he or she depended entirely on Sassy—now and for long into the future.

The reality of that meant she would need extra income. Not just for the first few months after the baby arrived, but for years to come. As of yet, she had no idea how she was going to deal with that problem. But, somehow, she would. For now, she wasn't going to worry about the financial ramifications. She simply wanted to relish the fact that she and the baby would be a family and she would do everything in her power to give it a good home.

She might not ever learn the truth of her own parentage, Sassy thought ruefully. But, at least, her own baby would know the truth. It would never have to doubt or wonder about the identity of its mother and father.

"Sassy! Sassy, where are you?"

Hearing Jett calling to her, Sassy turned away from the mirror.

"I'm in here, Jett. In the bedroom."

As she moved toward the clean clothes draped over the footboard of the bed, the door to her bedroom suddenly opened and she froze in her tracks, stunned to find herself staring straight at Jett.

"Jett!"

"Oh."

When he failed to shut the door and leave, Sassy grabbed up the clean jeans and clutched them in front of her.

"What are you doing?"

The question was inane, especially when she could see his gaze absorbing her like parched land sucking in sheets of rain.

His answer didn't come in the form of words, instead, he strode over and pulled her into the tight circle of his arms. The unexpected movement caused the jeans she'd been using for cover to slip to the floor.

"I'm doing what I've wanted to do since the first day we met," he muttered. "I'm making love to you."

Bracing her hands against his chest, the sensible side of her brain said to push him away, but the feel of his hands upon her bare skin and the warmth of his rock-hard body lured her closer to him instead.

And then the rational part of her shut down completely as Jett began to rain starved kisses over her face and lips, down her neck and then on the cleavage spilling over the cups of her bra.

"Sassy, Sassy."

Her name came out as a choked plea, and the angst in his voice tugged on her senses and drove a shaft of longing deep within her.

His lips hovering over hers, he said, "I know you want this as much as I do. Please tell me that."

"I do want you, Jett," she whispered thickly. "So very much."

His mouth lowered to hers, and as he kissed her over and over, something sweet pierced her, causing a river of pure emotion to flood through her until every cell in her body glowed with incredible pleasure.

They stood for long moments in that same spot, their mouths fused in an erotic feast, until the kiss was not nearly enough to quench the fire that had erupted between them.

With his hands at the sides of her waist, he guided her the few remaining steps to the bed and, with his mouth still fastened to hers, lowered her and himself onto the mattress. Once they were lying side by side, his hands were everywhere, gliding over her arms and legs, her face and hair, then finally her breasts.

The barrier of lace had him fumbling impatiently with the hook-and-eye closure at her back. When it finally parted, he peeled the garment away from her and tossed it to the floor. Then, with slow, agonizing leisure, his eyes admired the pale mounds and taut pink nipples before finally settling on her face.

"Saying you're beautiful would be silly of me, Sassy. You're beyond that. You're like an exotic island with soft white sand, bright blue skies and the scent of flowers wafting on the sea breeze."

No man had ever said such things to her, much less a man with a voice sexy enough to melt her bones.

A blush spread over her face. "Jett, you must have knocked your head on something out in the barn. You've lost your vision and your mind."

His fingers pushed into her hair and cradled the back of her head. "I've lost something," he agreed. "And you're the reason, Sassy."

Dizzied by his nearness, her hands curled over his shoulders. "You're not supposed to be here in my bed."

One corner of his lips crooked upward. "Then we'll go get into mine."

She couldn't fight him. Not when her body was already humming with delicious anticipation and her heart was singing a song of joyous surrender.

Sliding her hands downward, she began to pull apart the snaps on his denim shirt. "Let's not waste the time."

The descent of his head toward hers paused, and Sassy saw the same odd look appear in his eyes that she'd seen in the dry gulch after she'd dealt with the newborn calf.

Compelled by the look in his eyes, she whispered, "Is something wrong, Jett? If you've decided you don't want to have sex with a pregnant woman, I'll understand."

A squint narrowed his eyes and then he shook his head. "Nothing is wrong, Sassy. Nothing at all."

Wanting to believe him, she pulled his head down, and as his lips found hers, she refused to think about love or tomorrow. She didn't want to ruin what happiness she could find in his arms tonight.

Chapter 10

He wasn't supposed to want this much, feel this much. Sassy wasn't going to be staying. She was pregnant with another man's baby. He wasn't ready to be a family man. Getting involved with her complicated his relationship with the Calhouns. Yet even as these troubling thoughts tumbled through Jett's head, he couldn't stop his freefalling emotions or the heated desire that was consuming his body.

Sassy's pale skin was like smooth cream upon his tongue and the warm eagerness with which she caressed and kissed him intoxicated his senses to the point that he hardly knew what he was doing to her or she to him. The only thing he was aware of was that if he didn't connect his body to hers soon, he was going to die from the wanting.

Finally he managed to pull away from her long enough to jerk off his boots, and while he shed his clothing, Sassy slipped the panties over her hips and tossed them onto the heap his jeans had made on the floor.

Back on the bed, he aligned his body with hers and they reached for each other at the same time. And as the fronts of their bodies pressed close, the connection of bare flesh caused a flare of sizzling sparks that set fire to Jett's senses.

"Are you sure this is okay? You're up to this?" he asked.

Her answer was to slip her arm around his waist and thread one long, silky leg between his. "I'm fine. This is fine," she murmured.

Easing his head back, he looked into her blue eyes, searching for any sign of hesitation or regret. Even though his body was throbbing to connect with hers, he'd force himself to get up and walk away if she had doubts.

But he didn't detect any qualms on her face. Instead the warm lights flickering in her eyes sent hot arrows piercing right through him. Her fingers skimmed over his hair, dropped to his shoulder, then took a tantalizing stroll down to his chest. As she traced one brown nipple with the tip of her forefinger, Jett fought to hold on to his composure.

"Come here, Red," he choked, "and let me love you."

She tilted her mouth up to his, and as Jett kissed her an array of passions and desires burst to life, blinding him with their intensity. His heart and mind were like empty vessels and only now, in Sassy's arms, were they starting to fill, starting to learn what it was like to really feel and want and need.

He could sense her desire climbing at the same rapid rate as his, and with a needy groan, he rolled her beneath him. Then, planting his hands on either side of her head, he braced himself over her.

Her face was flushed, her fiery hair fanned above her head. The moist curve of her lips was like a sweet confection, luring him to dip his head and take a bite. He was slowly lowering his head to do just that when their gazes met, causing him to pause. The tender, giving light he saw in her blue eyes made his chest swell with something so big, so powerful that it forced the air from his lungs. Fear sliced through him, and for one split second he considered bolting from the bed and running as far and fast as he could from this redheaded siren in his arms. But his body refused to listen to the warning bells clanging in his head, it was too far gone to leave the paradise it had found.

"Jett. My darling Jett."

Her legs opened to welcome him inside and it was impossible for Jett to hold back any longer. He entered her slowly and gently, until her moist heat surrounded him completely. The sheer ecstasy of having his body connected to hers snapped his head back, while beneath him, he heard a moan of pleasure vibrating deep in her throat.

The next thing he knew she had his face cradled between her hands, drawing him down to her. When he found her mouth once again, the intimate contact sent his mind spinning, his body driving into hers.

She matched his movements with the same reckless need as her hips thrust urgently up to meet him, her tongue tangled with his.

Like a fierce wind, he was caught up in something so strong and overpowering that he became a lost particle, sailing and whirling with nothing to anchor him but her hot, sweet body.

Somewhere in the back of his mind, he registered the sensation of her soft hands gliding across his shoulders and back, gripping his arms, then cupping around his buttocks. The need for oxygen forced him to lift his mouth from hers, but as soon as he hauled in enough air to keep him going, he wasted no time in finding her lips again. He had to keep tasting her, had to sup her sighs and feel her warm breath whispering against his cheeks.

She was driving him up a wild, winding road at such a speed there was no way he could avoid the crash that was sure to come at the top. Still, he fought to slow the journey and keep the thrilling ride going. But the frantic writhing of her body was pushing him higher and higher, shoving him to the very peak of the mountain.

When he took the final plunge, she immediately followed and suddenly he was soaring somewhere in a darkened sky, flying among the stars with Sassy in his arms.

The sensation was so perfect, so all-consuming he wondered if he was dying. And then, somehow, he managed to force his lungs to breathe and to remind his heart that it needed to keep beating.

Collapsing beside her, he sucked in long harsh breaths and waited for his scattered senses to drift back to earth. Eventually he became aware of Sassy's heated body curled into his side, and the rapid rise and fall of her breasts told him that she was equally spent.

Eventually, she was the first to stir, and through hazy eyes he watched her prop her head on one bent elbow and shove a swathe of tangled hair off her face. When her blue eyes finally settled on his face, he found himself wondering if he was seeing an angel or another type of ethereal creature. She had to possess some sort of magical allure, he thought. There was no other explanation for the astonishing journey she'd just taken him on.

Unless it could be love. Was that what real love felt like? he wondered dazedly. He'd never experienced anything like that in his life— How could he know?

"Are you okay?"

Her quietly spoken question had him trying to chuckle, but the sound came out more like a weary groan. "Aren't I supposed to be asking you that question?"

A sweet smile tilted the corners of her swollen lips, and Jett was shocked to feel desire already starting to stir in his loins again. Now that he'd experienced the pleasure of her body, how could he ever get enough?

She said, "I don't know the protocol of these situations." Sighing, she lowered her head to rest her cheek upon his shoulder. "With me being pregnant, I suppose that sounds ridiculous, doesn't it?"

Reaching over, he rested a hand on her lower belly. The baby would come in late spring when the sage started to bloom and the winds grew warm. Would he be able to see the child? Hold it in his arms? Or would she be long gone by then? These past few days the questions had been on his mind, and now they left a heavy feeling in the middle of his chest.

"You've already explained how that happened. And the fact that you're carrying a baby inside of you only makes you more womanly in my eyes."

Her eyelids drifted downward as her hand moved gently over chest. "Well, you've proved me to be a liar."

His fingertips stroked across her damp forehead. "Hmm. What did you lie about?"

"I promised that I wouldn't let you get me into bed. Yet here I am."

"I didn't plan for this to happen tonight, Sassy. Not like this. But when I saw you standing there, looking like a goddess in white lace, I had to touch you."

She opened her eyes and gazed thoughtfully at his face. "Jett, this evening when we were out on the range, after I helped the calf, you looked at me in such a strange way. Were you angry about something?"

His fingers delved into her hair and combed through the silky strands that were spread out over the bedcover. "I wasn't angry. I was, I guess, stunned. When I saw you working over that calf, I realized that there's still so much about you that I've not yet learned."

"Well, you must have been stunned when I invited you to make love to me," she reasoned. "Because you had that same strange look on your face then."

He closed his eyes and tried not to think too much, feel too much. This evening, on the range, he'd seen for himself that Sassy was good for his kind of life. She wasn't timid or clingy. She was strong and beautiful and caring. And during the days she'd been so sick, she'd still remained positive and determined to get well. How could he continue to convince himself that she wasn't the perfect woman for him? That she didn't belong in his house and in his arms forever?

"I hadn't expected you to give in, Sassy. You'd vowed you wouldn't go to bed with me. Not unless love was involved." His hand stilled in her hair and he opened his eyes to look at her. "Are you thinking that I—I've had a change of heart?"

As soon as the awkward question had passed his lips, she drew away from him and sat up on the side of the bed. Confused by her withdrawal, Jett watched her reach for her clothes.

"Don't worry. Just because I caved in and went to bed with you doesn't mean I've gotten flowery ideas about the two of us."

Stung by that comment, he stared at her back. "Then why did you go to bed with me?"

Holding her sweater to her breasts, she twisted around to look at him. "Because I wanted to."

It wasn't the response he'd wanted or even expected to hear. "That doesn't sound like you, Sassy. But I guess tonight I'm learning some new things about you."

She shrugged. "Women are no different

from men, Jett. And I realized there's nothing wrong with me enjoying sex without strings."

Jett supposed he should be silently shouting with relief that she wasn't falling all over him and tearfully declaring her love. He didn't want that. Just as she'd said, he wanted sex without strings, too. Yet hearing her say it made it sound all wrong, made it feel all wrong.

"Well, I guess I should be happy you've gotten over all that sentimental stuff," he said stiffly.

"That's right. We have a fiery attraction to each other. That's all there is to it. And you've made me see that, while I'm here, there's nothing wrong with us enjoying the chemistry. Is there?"

The more she said, the worse it sounded, Jett thought. But to point that out to her would only make him look like an idiot and ultimately make her angry in the process. So he went along with her.

"No. Not a thing," he said in a thin voice.

She started to move away from the bed, but a spurt of frustration had him reaching for her arm and tugging her back onto the bed. "If that's the way you feel, then we need to make the most of every moment. Don't you think?"

Hesitancy flickered in her eyes, but then her features softened, and with a gentle smile on her face, she scooted closer and wrapped her arms around him.

"You're right again," she murmured.

Sex. That's all it had been and all it ever would be, Jett thought. And that had to be enough. For the both of them.

By the end of the week, Sassy realized she was in deep trouble. Going to bed with Jett had given her joys beyond anything she could have imagined. In his arms she felt like a princess being adored by her charming prince.

Maybe a year ago that would have been enough for her. She would've probably even believed that what she and Jett were sharing in bed would eventually lead to love and marriage. But the changes in her life this past year had left her older and wiser. She wasn't a fool. She understood that Jett couldn't love. Or if he could, he wouldn't allow it.

Now, the more time she spent in Jett's bed, the more she was growing to love him. It was a hopeless situation. One that was only going to get worse.

With a wistful sigh, she climbed down

from the corral fence where she'd been feeding pieces of carrots to two sorrel mares. "That's all, girls," she told the horses. "You'll have to wait for Jett to give you your supper."

Starting away from the corral, she caught the sound of an approaching vehicle, and when Bella's little economy car bounced over the hill toward the house, Sassy didn't know whether she was disappointed or relieved. With the woman back home, she and Jett would have to contain their desire or sneak to each other's bedrooms in the middle of the night.

Bella parked beneath the carport and was greeting Mary and Max when Sassy walked up to join her.

"Welcome home," Sassy called to her.

Turning on her slender high heels, Bella laughed and waved. "Oh, Sassy, hi! I didn't see you."

"I've been down at the corral feeding the mares a few treats. I saw you coming. Let me help you with your bags."

Bella opened the trunk. "Thanks. This one is lightest," she handed a small duffel bag to Sassy. "I don't think it's too heavy for a pregnant woman."

They entered the house through the front

entrance and Sassy followed Jett's sister down the hallway to her bedroom.

"Gosh, it's good to be home," Bella said.

She propped her rolling suitcase against the footboard of the bed and Sassy placed the duffel bag alongside the suitcase.

"It's good to have you home," Sassy told her, and meant it. She liked Bella very much. Not because she was Jett's sister, but because she was caring and thoughtful, and treated Sassy as an old and dear friend. "How was your trip?"

Bella groaned. "Long and tiring. But the case is over and our client won, so I can't complain." She looked at Sassy and smiled. "So, what's been going on around here? I got two short text messages from Jett while I was gone and they told me very little. One was something about a calf being born and the other one was to make sure I'd paid the electric bill."

Hoping she didn't look as sheepish as she felt, Sassy smiled. "Well, there hasn't been much going on. A new calf was born," she told Bella. "And Finn and I did get the DNA test started."

"Oh. That's exciting. I want to hear all about it." Bella sat on the edge of the bed and kicked off her heels. "Just let me change clothes and freshen up first."

Sassy nodded. "Take your time. I'll go make coffee."

Several miles away, Jett was leaving the Silver Horn ranch house after spending the past two hours helping Orin sift through more old family documents. Other than the unexplained checks that Orin had found the other day, they'd not run across anything else that looked remotely suspicious, and Jett was beginning to wonder if he and the Calhouns, barring Bart, had jumped to the wrong conclusions. Could be that Bart's reaction to Sassy was nothing more than him being a bastard, that her resemblance to the family was merely coincidental and that the checks actually were for cash.

Was that how he wanted it to be? To find that Sassy belonged to some other family hundreds of miles away from him and Carson City? Oh, God, he didn't know what he wanted anymore. Making love to Sassy this past week had changed everything. He felt as if he'd been taken by the bootheels and shaken.

She was eight years younger. That wasn't

a huge chasm between their ages, but it was enough to make him stop and consider the problems it might cause. But then why was he "considering" anything, he asked himself. Ever since she'd come to Carson City, she'd been telling him her plans were to return to her hometown of Ruidoso and make a home for herself and the baby. So far, she was sticking to that plan, no matter the outcome of the DNA test. And he could understand why. The Cantrells were wealthy and Sassy was clearly more to them than a maid. No doubt they would help her with any endeavor, whether that was getting a home or an education, or acquiring ranch property. She had friends who would help her get through the pregnancy and be there after her baby was born. So she hardly needed Jett. That meant marriage would be the only thing to hold her, he thought dismally. And he wasn't ready for that.

The insanity of his marriage to Erica had stained every part of his heart and mind. Even after the divorce, it had taken him months before he could step into the house without expecting to hear crying or yelling. It had taken much, much longer before he could look at a woman without feeling cold and sick, before talking to a woman didn't make him prepare for an argument when he got home. For five long years he'd convinced himself that living alone was all for the best. He didn't need a woman in his life. And he especially didn't need to put his heart on the chopping block again.

But now, day by day, hour by hour, it was becoming clear to Jett that any kind of life without Sassy in it would be boring and empty. Did that mean he already loved her?

Love. *Love.* Damn it, Jett was so sick of the word he wished he could wipe it from his mind. And though Sassy had never even whispered anything closely resembling the word, it popped into his mind each time he laid eyes on her.

She was using reverse psychology on him, Jett told himself as he jerked open the driver's door of his truck. She was deliberately avoiding the subject just to make him focus on it. So why wasn't he strong enough to resist her ploy?

Jett didn't want to even think about the answer to that question as he climbed behind the wheel and started the engine.

He was reaching for the gearshift when he

noticed Finn quickly striding across the small graveled parking area to intercept him.

Jett rolled down the window and waited for the young man.

"Jett, I stopped by the office but Kim said you were up here with Dad. Got a minute?"

"Sure. What's on your mind?

"Sassy." Finn pulled off his aviator glasses. "My brothers and I would like for you to bring her over one evening to have dinner with us—soon. Think you can talk her into coming?"

Even though it was clear that Finn felt a connection to Sassy, he'd not expected all the brothers to want to include her in a family gathering. Especially since they didn't know yet if she was a Calhoun. Not to mention that it would cause an uproar with Bart.

Jett frowned. "And risk having Bart threaten her again? I doubt it. I'm not so sure I'd want to subject her to that again."

Finn muttered a curse word. "Grandfather is going to have to get used to the idea of Sassy being around. And she might as well get used to him."

For some reason, Jett wasn't wild about Finn's suggestion. He didn't want to give Bart a chance to rip into her again. And if he was being completely honest with himself, he didn't want to share her company. Not with the Calhouns or Bella or anybody.

Dear God, was he becoming as obsessive and crazy as Erica had been?

No, Jett thought. He'd simply changed. Seeing after Sassy during those long days she'd suffered with nausea opened his eyes about caring for a sick woman. Instead of growing disgusted and weary with the situation, he'd wanted to ease Sassy's misery. He'd wanted to do anything and everything to make her feel better. No matter how long it took. Was that because he loved her? Really loved her?

Pushing the question out of his mind, he said, "Sassy is pregnant. She doesn't need to get upset."

Finn arched a dubious brow at him. "Hmm. For some reason you're sounding mighty protective of our little redbird."

Jett believed he was too old and jaded to blush, but the thought of all the sweet, delicious things he'd done to that little redbird these past few nights was enough to spread a wash of heat over his face.

"Finn, I was dealing with Sassy long before any of you met her. I feel…responsible for her. There's nothing peculiar about that."

"No," Finn said with slow thoughtfulness. "Nothing peculiar about a man like you falling for a beautiful woman like her, either."

Jett opened his mouth to protest, but just as quickly clamped his jaw shut. What was the point in trying to hide this fascination he had for Sassy? It was probably written all over his face anyway.

"Okay, I'll admit it, Finn, I have…grown fond of Sassy."

Finn's grin was broad and suggestive. "Fond? That's a weak word to attach to a woman as special as Sassy."

Jett would have expected Finn to be all-knowing about horses, but he'd not expected him to have such wisdom about women. *Fond* was far too weak a word to describe the way he felt about Sassy. He felt torn, consumed and exhilarated. Mix all those things together and you create one crazy man.

He was staring out the windshield, wondering how he was going to come up with a sensible reply when Finn reached in and slapped a hand on Jett's shoulder. "I'm sorry, Jett. I didn't mean to pry. But each time you say her name I can see a spark in your eyes."

Jett groaned. "Go ahead and say it, Finn. I'm a fool."

Finn remained quiet for so long that Jett swung his gaze back to the younger man.

"Jett, I still remember what a bad time you went through with Erica. We all remember it. But that's done and over. It's time you started believing again."

"Believing in what, Finn?"

"Yourself, for starters."

The young cowboy's words hit Jett like a brick. Was that what he'd done? Stopped believing he could make the right choices? That he could ever have or keep a real woman by his side?

Blowing out a heavy breath, Jett pulled the gearshift into reverse. "I'll think about that, Finn. And I'll talk to Sassy about the dinner. She might agree to meeting out somewhere or we could all meet at my house."

"I'll leave that up to you and her. Thanks, Jett," Finn told him, then stepped back and waved him off.

Three hours later, when Jett arrived home, he groaned out loud when he spotted Bella's car parked beneath the carport. He'd expected his sister to be gone for at least one more day. Her unexpected arrival was definitely going to put a kink in his plans.

Parking the truck, he glanced down at the

bouquet of flowers lying in the passenger seat. If he took them into the house, Bella would see them and start asking questions. And Sassy would probably assume he'd gotten them for his sister's homecoming. She'd never expect the flowers were for her.

The thought put a grimace on Jett's face. These past few days he'd taken and taken from Sassy. Mainly because he'd been so empty before she'd come into his life that he'd needed so much to fill him up. But it was past time he started giving back to her. And he wanted to start by convincing her that Nevada and the J Bar S were her home.

Entering the house through the kitchen, he spotted Sassy alone at the stove stirring something in a saucepan. The minute she heard him coming through the door, she looked around and gave him a bright smile. Suddenly all the qualms he'd had earlier flew out of his mind.

"Hi, Jett. Did you see that Bella is home?"

Not bothering to remove his hat, he strode quickly over to her. "I did. Where is she?"

"In the living room, making calls, I think."

He glanced over his shoulder to make sure his sister hadn't walked into the room.

"Good." He curled a hand around her arm. "Come with me."

"Jett! My icing is—"

"Turn off the burner. I want to get out of here before Bella interrupts us!"

She did as he asked, and on the way out the door grabbed her jacket. As they walked, she pushed her arms into the sleeves.

"Jett, what in the world are you doing? Why all this hurry? Won't we have plenty of time to check on the cattle after we eat?"

This past week, Sassy had taken to going out with him in the evenings to check on the cattle. It had become a special time for Jett. To have Sassy at his side as he surveyed his land and livestock made everything feel right and good.

"Noah is feeding and checking on the herd this evening. I have something else in mind for you—us. Just wait."

"All right. I quit with the questions," she said. "I'm just wondering what Bella is going to think when she walks through the house and can't find me."

He pulled a cell phone from a leather holder on his belt and scrolled down until he found the correct number, then tossed the instrument over to her. "Text her and explain we've gone for a drive and will be home later. That ought to be enough."

As she dealt with the phone, Jett drove them away from the barn area and turned the truck west on a brushy track that led them upward through low, undulating hills scattered with thick chaparral, tufts of sage and dried Indian rice grass.

Sassy remained quiet as she gazed out the window at the passing landscape and Jett was grateful that she'd stopped asking him about where they were going. He needed these moments to gather his thoughts and hopefully form the right words that he needed to say to her.

The road abruptly narrowed as they passed through a fold in the hills. As they emerged on the other side, wide open spaces were suddenly upon them and they were looking at a sea of Joshua trees bathed in a pink-and-purple sunset.

"Oh!" Sassy gasped, as she stared raptly out the windshield. "I've never seen anything more beautiful, Jett! Please, stop. I want to get out and look."

He braked the truck to a stop in the middle of the track. "That's what I was planning to do."

She looked over at him in surprise. "Is this why you were in such a hurry? You wanted me to see this place right at sunset?"

He smiled sheepishly. "This is one of my favorite spots on the ranch. I wanted to bring you to see it. The sunset just happened to be here."

"I'm thrilled that it was!" Shooting him a dazzling smile, she jerked open the door and scurried to the ground.

While she went to stand in front of the truck, Jett lifted the flowers from the backseat, then carefully hid them behind his back as he walked around to join her. She immediately snuggled close to his side, and in that moment, Jett realized that this woman and her child were meant to be in his life. But would she see it that way?

"You know what I'm thinking?" she asked, while gazing with appreciation at the view in front of them.

"No. Tell me."

"That this ranch of yours is so different from what I first thought." She glanced over at him. "And so are you. When I first saw you, I thought you were a lawyer disguised as a cowboy. Now I realize you're more of a cowboy than a lawyer. I think you're far more connected to this land than you are to your desk."

"I'm glad you realize that, Sassy, because—" He broke off and, using his free hand, gestured to the wild expanse of ground stretching toward the blaze of sunset. "I want this ranch to belong to you, too."

She turned a look of confusion on him. "What did you say? Something about belonging?"

Pulling the bouquet from behind his back, he presented the fragrant blooms to her. "That's right, Sassy. I want you to belong to me and me to you. I want this ranch to be ours. I'm asking you to marry me."

Chapter 11

Sassy stared in stunned silence at the pink asters and yellow lilies intertwined with delicate baby's breath. She'd just been telling herself not to read anything romantic into this little trip to view the Joshua trees and the gorgeous sunset. Jett wasn't that type of man. He was thoughtful, but not dreamy.

But apparently he, or she, or the both of them were dreaming now, she thought wildly.

"Marry? Jett—I don't understand. What am I supposed to say?"

"A simple yes is all I need."

Her head was suddenly reeling with pictures of the future. In so many ways, being

Jett's wife would be incredible. There was no doubt in her mind that he would be a good and faithful husband. And the financial security he would provide for her and the baby was beyond anything she could have imagined in her life. A woman probably shouldn't expect more than that from a man. But she wanted more. Much more.

Dropping her nose to the cluster of flowers, she drew in the sweet scent before she faced him. "Why now, Jett? You've told me more than once that you didn't want to get married again."

Moving closer, he wrapped his arms around her until the flowers were very nearly squashed between them. "This week with you has made me see things differently, Sassy. We fit together. We understand each other. And I can provide a good home for you and the baby."

A woman should feel joy when the man she loves proposes to her, but at this very second Sassy's chest was filled with a heavy ache. "So, in other words, we'd have a great marriage of convenience."

Beneath the brim of his hat, she saw his dark brows arch with surprise and then her eyes settled on his chiseled lips. The sight of them infused her with longing and deep regret.

"That's not exactly how I think of it. But if you want to put it that way…" he said slowly.

She swallowed hard before she could manage to push the next words past her tight throat. "Well, thanks for the offer, but I'm not interested."

He stared at her for long moments as all around them the light from the setting sun quickly faded into twilight. In the far distance a hawk shrieked as it swooped at its prey.

"Why?" he wanted to know. "Am I wrong in thinking that you feel something for me?"

Her eyes filled with misty tears. "You're not wrong at all. And that's exactly why I have to turn down your proposal. Because I do feel something for you. I love you, Jett."

It was clear she'd shocked him. His face went pale, and he took a step back as though she'd literally shoved him.

"Oh, Sassy," he said, in an anguished voice. "Why did you have to bring that into things?"

"And why did you *not* bring it into things?" she asked angrily. Then, shaking her head, she looked away from him and drew in several bracing breaths. "I'm sorry, Jett. This is all my fault. I was wrong—I've been wrong for several days now. I led you to believe that all I wanted from you was sex. Because I understood that's how you wanted things to be with us. And I've been able to pretend. But, now that you've asked me to marry you, I can't pretend any longer. I can't—I won't—enter into a marriage without love."

She started toward the truck door, only to have him put a hand on her shoulder. "You're not thinking sensibly right now, Sassy. You're thinking with your heart instead of your head. And that is never the wise thing to do. I can provide your baby with everything it will need to grow into a fine young man or woman. Isn't that what you want for your child?"

He didn't understand. How could he? His heart was too wrapped up in armor to be able to see or feel real love.

"I've managed to make it on my own up until now, Jett. And providing for a child doesn't necessarily make you a parent. It needs warmth and love. And yes, there's that word again. But don't worry. That's the last time you're going to hear it from me."

Pulling away from him, she jerked open the door and climbed back into the vehicle, leaving him no choice but to follow.

As he turned the truck around and drove back to the ranch house, she stared out the window and wondered what she was going to do now. There was no way she could continue staying under the same roof with Jett. Now that they had both put their feelings out in the open, it would simply be agony.

"Looks like I've ruined your evening," he said gruffly. "I'll remember that the next time I get the idea to propose marriage to a woman."

"You haven't ruined my evening." He'd just ruined everything, she thought dismally. Their time together had been precious. But the few days of fairy tale had come to an end. "Seeing the Joshua trees and the sunset was something I'll never forget."

She gazed down at the pink and yellow blooms lying in the crook of her arm and her throat ached with tears. "I'm sorry you wasted the flowers. You can give them to Bella." She looked over at him and tried to smile. "Deep down you don't want to get married, Jett. You haven't really thought this through. What it would mean to have me and a baby on the ranch. You'd be tied down and start feeling trapped like you did with Erica. Later on you'll be glad that I had enough sense to turn you down."

He stared straight ahead and Sassy could tell by the tautness of his jaw that he was more than a little upset. Which didn't make much sense, considering that he didn't love her. But then, there wasn't a man alive who liked to hear no from a woman, she silently reasoned.

He said, "You know how to make a guy feel real worthwhile, Sassy."

There were many retorts she could have made, but she didn't. She'd never liked arguing. Especially when it was obvious that cross words wouldn't change the situation.

When they returned to the house, Bella was in the kitchen, adding the last touches to the meal of lasagna that Sassy had put in the oven before Jett arrived home.

"Well, there you two are." She turned away from the cabinet and immediately spotted the flowers in Sassy's arms. "Wow! Where did you get those? They're beautiful!"

Using all the acting ability she possessed, Sassy smiled and carried the flowers over to the other woman. "I sent Jett a text message telling him you'd come home, so he stopped and got you these. Thoughtful brother, huh?"

Bella's mouth flopped open as she looked past Sassy's shoulder to where her brother was shrugging out of his ranch coat.

"Jett, what in the world has Sassy been feeding you? Whatever it is, it's softened up your tough old hide!" Taking the flowers from Sassy, she hurried over to her brother and gave him an affectionate kiss on the cheek. "Thank you, Jett. With Sassy here, I wouldn't have thought you'd miss me this much."

Smiling wanly, he gave her a one-armed hug. "Forget it, sis. Enjoy the flowers."

Later that evening, Jett was sitting in a little room situated at the back of the house that he used as an office when Bella knocked and stepped through the open doorway.

"Busy?" she asked.

He shook his head. "Not exactly. Just catching up on some things." He switched off the computer while his sister rested her hip on the corner of the desk. "I figured you'd already hit the sack. From everything you told us at dinner, you've had a long and trying week in the courtroom. I hope Adam appreciates your dedication."

"My boss pays me nicely. And I'll get

rested up. In fact I'm on my way to bed now. I just wanted to check on you and say good-night."

Apparently Bella had already sensed that he wasn't fine. That's why she'd felt compelled to look in on him. "I'm okay."

She pulled a pen from a wooden box and rolled it between her fingers. "You didn't say much at supper. Sassy wasn't talking, either."

"Guess we're all talked out."

"Hmm. Must have been pretty boring without me this week."

He kept his eyes directed at the messy desktop. "It wasn't the same."

From the corner of his eye, he could see her folding her arms across her chest and studying him with a bothered expression.

"Those flowers weren't for me, were they?"

He wiped a hand over his face. He loved his sister and appreciated that she was concerned about him, but right now he was breaking apart. His brain, his body, every cell inside him was on fire with a pain he couldn't fathom, much less stem.

"How did you guess?"

"Sassy's a terrible liar. And you've never bought me a flower in your life."

He blew out a heavy breath. "That's another mistake I've made. You're the best sister that any guy could have. I should let you know from time to time."

Bella groaned. "Oh, Jett," she softly scolded, "I don't need flowers or gifts from you to know how you feel about me. When something comes from the heart you don't have to keep expressing it in words or gifts. The other person just naturally feels it."

Using both hands, he raked his fingers through his hair while his aching brain considered Bella's sage remark. During his marriage to Erica he'd told her over and over that he loved her. He'd even surprised her with all sorts of gifts, including flowers. Yet she'd never truly believed him. Maybe that was because she'd recognized, even when he hadn't, that what he felt for her was something less than real love.

Now he was asking Sassy to enter the same sort of one-sided marriage, but she'd been smart enough to say no.

Deep down, you don't want to get married, Jett.... Later on you'll be glad that I had enough sense to turn you down.

Trying to shove Sassy's telling words out of his mind, he muttered, "Erica sure as hell never felt it from me. And I tried, Bella. God knows I tried."

Easing her hip off the edge of the desk, Bella moved around the piece of furniture to stand next to his chair. "Sassy isn't Erica." She placed a comforting hand on his shoulder. "Would you like to tell me what's happened between the two of you?"

"Maybe later. Right now I need to figure out how a man can cure himself of being a fool."

"He recognizes that life isn't perfect and that contracts can always be broken." Bending over, she placed a kiss on top of his head. "Good night, brother."

Nearly an hour later, Jett left his office with Bella's parting words still lingering in his jumbled thoughts and made his way to the front of the house to make sure everything was secured for the night.

When he walked into the living room to turn off the lights, he found Sassy sitting quietly in front of the fireplace. Since they'd returned home from the Joshua trees, he'd not talked to her alone. He wasn't sure he wanted to now, but since he was already halfway into the room, it would look cowardly of him to walk away without a word.

"I wasn't expecting you to be up. I just came in to turn off the lights," he said stiffly.

She immediately rose to her feet. "Go ahead. I need to go to my room, anyway."

Without him. For the first night in five nights he wouldn't be lying next to her in bed. He wouldn't be touching her soft skin or have her arms holding him close, her body warming his. It was going to be a long and painful night.

He walked past her to shut the wire mesh curtains of the fireplace. "Wait just a minute."

Behind him he could hear her release a heavy sigh.

"Jett, I'm sorry, but I don't want to talk any more tonight."

She started to walk off, but he quickly blocked her path. "I don't want to talk about you or me or us," he said. "This is something else."

She searched his face, and he wondered what she was seeing. The same man that Erica had seen so many years ago? He didn't want to be that man. But how did he go about changing?

"Okay, what is it?"

He said, "I talked with Finn this afternoon. He and his brothers want me to bring you over to the Horn for dinner one evening. Soon."

Her face remained stoic. "That's very nice of them, but I'm not sure I want to do that."

He asked, "Why? I thought you liked the Calhouns."

"I do like them. That's why I don't want to bring more trouble to their home."

He rolled his eyes. "My Lord, Sassy, you call having dinner with them trouble? Compared to a DNA test? That's rich!"

Her jaw tight, she stared off at a shadowed corner of the room. "If I remember right, you were just as anxious for me to do that test as Finn was. Now you're throwing it up to me as though I'm some sort of fortune hunter." Her lips pressed to a thin line, she turned back to him. "You're the Calhoun lawyer. Go write up a statement right now so that I can sign it. I want to make sure everyone, especially you, will see that I won't take a precious cent from them. No matter what the outcome of the DNA test is!"

He muttered a curse under his breath. "Why are you— This was supposed to be about having one simple dinner. Why have you gone off on this crazy tangent?"

Turning her back to him, she shook her head. "I'm sorry, Jett. This hasn't exactly been a pleasant evening for either of us. I'm feeling a little raw and—"

"A little raw!" he practically yelled. With a hand on her arm, he whirled her back to him. "Woman, I'm more than a little raw! You've ripped me apart!"

She stared at him. "Why are you so cut up? Because we're not going to have sex tonight? Or ever again? That shouldn't be ripping you apart. Not when there're plenty of women around who'd be more than willing to take my place. After all, you're not interested in love—just marriage."

Her flippant response was the last straw when it came to Jett's flimsy composure. Before he could anticipate his own intentions, he snatched her tight against him and covered her mouth with his.

She didn't resist, and for long moments Jett feasted on her lips and tried to store away the pleasures that only she could give him.

When, eventually, she ripped her mouth from his, Jett buried his face in the side of her hair. "I don't want any other woman, Sassy. I want you."

With a muffled cry, she tore away from him and without giving him a second glance, raced out of the room. Jett watched her go and wondered if the heavy weight in his chest would ever leave.

Throughout the week, Sassy did her best to forge ahead and pretend that everything was great, especially in front of Bella. So far, she'd not had the heart to tell the other woman about Jett's proposal. Mainly because she wasn't certain what Bella would think about her brother marrying a woman he'd only met a few weeks ago. A woman, moreover, who was carrying another man's baby.

The coming child was the only thing left of Barry, and Sassy hoped that when she located his father up in Colorado that the man would be pleased with the news of the baby. At least her child would have one grandfather.

As for Jett, she couldn't guess what he'd been thinking or feeling this past week. Mostly he'd been avoiding her company, and when they were thrown together he was quiet and moody. So far he'd not reiterated the invitation for them to dine at the Silver Horn, and Sassy was content to let the subject drop. Although she would love to see Finn and his brothers again, she didn't want to go anywhere near Bart. Not that she was afraid of the man. Far from it. But as she'd attempted to tell Jett, she didn't want to cause upheaval in the family. Even if it was just over a simple dinner. She'd decided the best thing to do would be to call Finn and ask him to meet her somewhere in town for lunch.

"Hello, Sassy. Are you out for an afternoon stroll?"

At the sound of Noah's voice, Sassy looked across the ranch yard to see the cowboy standing near the open door of the barn, saddling a big red roan.

Waving a greeting at the man, she changed direction and walked over to him and the horse.

"The weather is much warmer today, and I needed to get out of the house for a while." The collies sat on their haunches at her side and she reached to stroke their shiny heads. During her time here on the ranch, she'd grown very attached to the dogs, and they to her. It was going to break her heart to eventually say goodbye to them. "What are you going to do with the roan? Move cattle?"

He fastened the end of the girth to its holder on the saddle. "No. Ride fence."

"Oh, that sounds nice. Can I tag along?" She'd not had the chance to ride since she'd left the Chaparral and that was over three weeks ago. Before Jett had proposed his marriage of convenience, she'd planned to ask him to take her riding on one of his days off. But now she wouldn't ask him for the time of day.

The big man tossed a coiled lariat over the saddle horn, then turned to face her. "I'm not so sure about that, Sassy," he said with reservations. "You're with child and—"

She waved away his words before he could finish. "The doctor said it would be fine for me to ride. As long as I don't tire myself and am careful not to fall."

"To be honest, Sassy, I don't think Jett would like it."

She bristled. "What's Jett got to do with it? There's nothing wrong with me riding a horse across the pasture!"

He thought for a long moment before a crafty smile spread across his face. "Okay. I'd like the company. I'll saddle Rascal for you. He has two gears. Slow and slower."

"Great," she told him. "While you get Rascal ready, I'll go change into my boots."

For the next hour they rode along a fence that ran due north from the house. Rascal, the black horse that Noah had saddled for her, was a sweet-natured animal that clopped along at a leisurely pace and followed Sassy's commands without any protest.

From the few times she'd been in the man's company, she'd quickly concluded that Noah was not a talker. So, as they rode along, she'd not expected him to hold any sort of conversation. Other than making a comment here and there about a cow or calf or a piece of the fence, he said little. And that was fine with Sassy. At least she was out of the house and not staring at the walls, wondering what she was going to do about Jett.

Not that there was much she could do about the man. They were at loggerheads, and she'd come to the conclusion that the best thing she could do for herself and her child was to get back on a plane and head home to the Chaparral. At least her old job would be waiting and she'd be back among friends.

When they reached a windmill with a watering tank, they let the horses drink, then

Noah announced it was time they turned around and headed back to the house.

They were somewhere near a quarter of a mile away from their destination when Sassy spotted Jett's truck barreling toward them.

Noah said, "Looks like the boss is in a hurry."

The two of them continued moving forward until Jett pulled alongside them, and then they reined their horses to a halt.

Expecting him to roll down the window and speak to Noah, Sassy was surprised when he left the truck and walked over to her and Rascal.

"What are you doing?"

His incredulous tone had her frowning at him. "What does it look like? I'm out getting some fresh air and exercise. We've been riding fence line."

His jaw tightened. "What if you fall? What if the horse spooks and pulls a runaway?"

"Rascal? Pull a runaway?" Noah's chuckles said what he thought about that possibility.

Stunned that the other man came to her defense, she glanced over to see Noah's gloating grin.

Jett glared at him. "You're the one who let her do this! For two cents I'd fire your ass!"

Seemingly unruffled by Jett's threat, the hired hand reached into his jeans pocket, pulled out two pennies and tossed them at his boss.

"There. You have it. Go ahead and fire me."

Not saying another word to Noah, Jett grabbed the shank on Rascal's bit to prevent the horse from moving. "Come on," he ordered Sassy. "You're riding back to the house in the truck. Noah can lead Rascal home."

Flabbergasted, she said, "Not on your life! I'm riding Rascal back. Now turn loose of his bit!"

Instead of doing as she asked, he started to reach up and haul her off the horse, but Sassy quickly put a heel in Rascal's ribs and made the horse sidestep.

"Leave her be," Noah quietly warned Jett. "The lady knows what she wants. And right now, it ain't you."

She'd thought she'd seen Jett angry before, but clearly she'd never seen him looking like this, as though he could explode at any second.

"I'll see you at the barn," he growled at Noah, then he jumped in the truck and gunned it in the direction of home.

Sassy looked over at the hired hand. "This

is awful, Noah. Just awful. Why did you have to say all those things to him? You were making matters about a hundred times worse!"

Noah grinned. "I know. I did it on purpose."

She let out an incredulous gasp. "You what?"

He reined his horse close enough to pat her on the shoulder. "Don't worry, Sassy. I just gave Jett a little of what he's been needing. He'll get over it."

Still unconvinced, she shook her head. "But what if he really fires you?"

Noah chuckled. "I've been fired before. Now come on, we'd better get back to the O.K. corral. I got the feeling a shootout is about to happen."

Back at the barn, Jett angrily continued to heave bales of alfalfa into the back of the feed truck even though he'd far surpassed the daily ration. There was no way he'd let Sassy and his hired hand make a fool out of him again. As far as he was concerned, they could ride off into the sunset and never come back!

I need to figure out how a man can cure himself of being a fool.

He understands that life isn't perfect and contracts can always be broken.

The exchange he'd had with his sister popped into his brain just as a hay bale plopped with a heavy thud into the bed of the truck. And, with a mindless shake of his head, he dropped the hay hook and wiped a hand over his face.

What the hell was he doing? He wasn't a jealous, raving idiot. At least, he hadn't been until he'd come home and found Sassy and Noah out on the range. Seeing her enjoying herself with another man, even in a totally innocent way, had hit him hard. Even the fact that Mary and Max had joined them on the trip had seemed like a betrayal.

Sassy had told him that she loved him, and in spite of himself, Jett had clung to those three words these past few days while hoping and praying they'd be enough to make her stay and be a part of his life. But a lifeline needed a person at both ends to make it balanced and strong. Now he was beginning to see that he'd not put his whole heart and soul into his grip.

Dear God, out there on the range he'd been behaving just as maniacally as Erica had, he thought miserably. Is that what love did to a person?

The question had him grabbing a seat on

an overturned feed bucket and dropping his head into his hands. All this time he'd been fighting so hard not to love Sassy. Yet, all the while, he'd been falling in love with her more and more. Why hadn't he been able to see that and admit it before now, before he'd caused Sassy to throw up a cold wall between them?

The sound of hooves striking the hard earth had him looking up to see Noah and Sassy riding into the ranch yard. His first instinct was to run out to her, to beg her to forgive him for being such a blind, stubborn bonehead. But he needed to give her enough space to cool off and himself enough time to figure out how he was going to convince her that his heart was finally in the right place.

As soon as she climbed down from Rascal's saddle, she gave the reins to Noah, and after exchanging a few brief words with him, walked straight to the house. Once she was out of sight, Jett walked out to help the other man tend to the horses.

"Is she all right?" Jett asked as he glanced once again in the direction of the house.

Noah shot him a look of warning. "I don't think you ought to be asking her that right now. Her red hair is showing—she's hopping mad."

Jett groaned. "I've made a real mess of things, Noah."

"We all do from time to time. Forget it."

As they led the two horses inside the barn, Jett pulled two pennies from his jeans. "Here." He handed the coins to Noah. "I don't want these."

With a half grin, the other man stuffed the pennies into his shirt pocket. "I never thought that you did."

Noah's cocksure remark had Jett bursting out in laughter and giving his friend's shoulder a companionable shake. "C'mon, buddy, let's get these horses taken care of and then I'm going to go to the house and try to convince Sassy that I'm not the bastard she thinks I am."

"That's a pretty tall order. How do you plan to do it?" Noah asked.

Jett's expression instantly sobered. "Noah, do you know what happens to a marriage license when there's no love behind it?"

"You're asking the wrong guy."

"Well, I'll tell you what happens." He made a tearing motion with his hands. "You might as well rip it into tiny pieces before the I dos are ever spoken."

The other man looked highly skeptical.

"That's going to fix things with Sassy?" He shook his head. "I'm afraid it's gonna take a hell of a lot more than that to convince her."

"Not if I know Sassy."

Chapter 12

When Jett entered the house a few minutes later, he found Sassy removing her clothes from the closet and carefully folding them into her suitcase. The sight chilled him to the bone, but he didn't let it stop him from his purpose.

"Is this the way you want to resolve things, Sassy? By running away?"

She barely acknowledged him with a glance as she continued to pack her belongings. "I'm not running. I'm going home. Where I belong, I might add. Finn can contact me later with the results of the DNA test. I'm not sure I even care one way or the other anymore."

"You're only saying that out of anger at me. You do care. And this is your home. You belong here."

She merely grunted and quickened her pace. "Under the circumstances, I think it's best that we quit torturing each other. And the only way for me to make that happen is to get away from you."

He tried not to let her stiffly spoken words skewer him or change his course of action.

"Sassy," he said quietly, while cautiously reaching for her arm. "Sassy, darling, I'm sorry. I was totally out of line. More than that—I was wrong. I've been wrong for a long time."

When she refused to look at him, he took her by the shoulders and forced her to face him. By then tears were slipping onto her cheeks and he used his fingers to gently wipe them away.

She sniffed. "About what? Inviting me to stay here? For going to bed with me? I'm sure that right about now you're regretting a lot of things—especially ever meeting me!"

He didn't know how he could smile at a time like this. But finally recognizing the love he felt for Sassy had filled his heart with such joy that he couldn't contain it.

Fortunately, she didn't resist as he drew her against him and tucked her head into the curve of his shoulder. "The only thing I regret, Sassy, is not realizing how much you mean to me before now."

Her head jerked back and forth. "No. You're saying that just because I'm leaving!"

"I'm saying it because I mean it." He pointed to the bed. "And not because of a suitcase and a bunch of clothes piled on the bed."

"No," she said again, then turned her back to him. "It's too convenient, Jett. And way too late."

He tried not to let his heart sink. What he felt for Sassy was too precious to lose, and he would fight to his last breath to keep it and her and the baby. "I don't blame you for feeling that way, Sassy. I only ask that you give me time. Give me a chance to explain, and then I believe you'll understand."

She hesitated, her blue eyes dark with suspicion. "I'm not sure about this—or you—or anything anymore."

The fact that she wasn't refusing him flatout gave him a thread of hope. "Oh, Sassy, you can't imagine what these past few days have done to me. I want to—"

His words were suddenly interrupted by

the ring of his cell phone, but he paused for only a moment and shook his head. "I don't care who that is, we need to talk until this is settled."

The ringing stopped, but as he guided her over to the bed so that they could both sit down, the ringing began again.

Sassy sighed. "You'd better at least see who it is, Jett."

"Better than that. I'll turn the damned thing off." He pulled out the phone and just as he was about to push the off button, he noticed the call was from the Silver Horn. "Hmm. It's someone from the Horn. Do you want me to answer it?"

"Yes. Or the person will probably keep ringing until you answer," she told him.

Deciding Sassy was right, he swiped the phone. As soon as it landed against his ear and he heard Bart's voice, his mouth fell open with shock. He couldn't remember the last time Bart Calhoun called him after hours. Whatever the reason, it had to be something urgent.

"Jett, is that you?"

"Yes, this is Jett," he answered.

"Bart here. Is that woman there with you?"

That woman. He had to hold his tongue to

keep from cursing a blue streak at the man. Yet, at the same time, he wondered what was making the man behave so out of character. "Are you talking about Ms. Matthews?"

"What other woman would I be talking about?"

Jett searched for every bit of patience he could find. "Sassy is here. Why?"

"I want you to bring her over here to the Horn. I want to talk to her. Now!"

Jett turned an uncertain look on Sassy. "I—I'm not sure if she's up to it," he hedged. "What is this all about, anyway?"

There was long pause and Jett realized the man wasn't used to being questioned, especially by one of his employees.

"It's none of your business. This is between me and that woman. Just get her over here and I'll take care of the rest."

Jett opened his mouth to tell Bart to go to hell but the connection ended abruptly, cheating him out of the pleasure.

As he put the phone away, Sassy looked at him with concern. "What was that all about? Who were you talking to? You look like you want to wring someone's neck."

His mind whirling, Jett frowned. "That was Bart Calhoun. He wants to see you."

Clearly stunned, she pressed a hand to her throat. "Wants to see me?" she echoed. "Why? Do you think— Maybe Finn got the test results?"

"No. I have the feeling Finn and his brothers know nothing about this phone call. Bart sounded even more demanding and arrogant than his normal self. I hardly think he wants this meeting to welcome you into the family." Wrapping a bracing hand around her elbow, he asked, "What do you want to do? I was about to tell him to get lost, but he hung up on me. All you have to do is give me the word."

Sassy lifted her chin. "No. I'm going to face the man. It's probably what I should have done from the very beginning. If you can take me now, I'll change clothes and we'll be on our way."

He suddenly felt very anxious. For her and himself. Whatever affected Sassy's life affected his just as deeply, and he had no idea what this meeting with Bart would yield. "Whenever you're ready, I'll be waiting in the kitchen," he told her.

For some unexplainable reason, Sassy felt remarkably calm as, nearly an hour later, they entered the Silver Horn ranch house and climbed the stairs to Bart's study. She didn't know what the man wanted, and though Jett had intended to alert the rest of the family to this meeting, she'd asked him to wait. There would be plenty of time to talk to Orin, and Finn and his brothers after she learned what the Calhoun patriarch had on his mind.

After Jett knocked on the closed door, the two of them entered a room paneled in dark wood and furnished with oxblood leather furniture. Along one wall, heavy drapes were pulled aside, and a large window gave a view of dusk falling across a ridge of distant mountains.

Bart Calhoun was sitting behind a mahogany desk, and Sassy had to admit that for a man in his early eighties his appearance was impressive. Even at this advanced age, his shoulders were broad and strong, his salt-and-pepper hair was thick and wavy. A pair of tortoise-framed glasses were perched on the end of his nose and a whiskey tumbler filled with ice and amber-colored liquid occupied one hand. Clearly the man believed he was above following doctor's orders, or he wasn't the least bit worried about his blood pressure.

As they moved into the room, she felt Jett's arm settle against the back of her waist, and though she didn't know what was going to happen to their relationship once this meeting was over, his touch comforted her.

Not bothering with a greeting, Bart said, "I want to talk with Ms. Matthews alone, Jett. She doesn't need a lawyer at her side to hear what I have to say."

Jett's fingers tightened against her side as they came to a stop a few feet in front of the wide desk. "I'm not leaving Sassy in here alone with you, Bart. So get on with it."

Bart arched a brow at Jett. "You're sounding awful uppity for a man in your position, aren't you?"

"Call it what you want, Bart. I'm just saying it like it is."

"All right, I'll say it like it is," he retorted, his dark eyes boring a hole through Sassy. "I think it's time we put an end to this little matter."

Jett said, "I've wondered how long it was going to take before you decided to man up."

Bart's eyes narrowed on Jett. "What are you talking about?"

"Everybody has been wondering if you're developing dementia, but in my opinion, using that medical explanation for your behavior would be too kind. You're cunning and manipulative. You could have enlightened Sassy weeks ago about her parents. Instead, you'd rather play a hateful game of chess."

"I know what Sassy is interested in. The same thing her mother was interested in. And don't think that just because you have Finn and the rest of the family on your side means you can fool me. You think I don't know about that ridiculous DNA test?" He turned an accusing eye on Jett. "Or you and Orin digging through files like a pair of dirty moles? You two aren't going to find anything. There's nothing to find."

Shocked, Sassy stared at the old rancher. Could it really be true that he knew her mother? Or was the old man using some twisted ploy with her just because he didn't want her around?

Jett must have read her thoughts because he swiftly countered with a question. "How do you know what Sassy's mother was interested in? Were you acquainted with the woman?"

"You might be a lawyer, Jett, but I'm not on the witness stand." He looked straight at Sassy. "I want you to leave this area and never come back. I don't want you around Finn or any of my family."

Determined not to let him intimidate her,

Sassy moved closer to the old man's desk. Jett moved right along with her. "Whether I stay in Carson City or anywhere else is not your concern, Mr. Calhoun."

A smug sort of sneer came over Bart's face as he plopped down his drink and opened a drawer on the right side of the desk. When he pulled out an envelope and tossed it onto the ink blotter, Sassy and Jett exchanged a puzzled glance.

"This will help you to see things my way." He gestured to the envelope. "Take it, Ms. Matthews."

She did as he asked and for the first time in days her stomach took a sickening lurch. The check in her hands was more money than she could comprehend.

"What is this?" she asked curtly.

The older man belted back the last of his drink. "Just call it a thank-you for leaving Nevada and never contacting the Calhoun family again."

Jett leaned over the desk, and for one second Sassy feared he was going to grab the man by the throat. "What is your problem, Bart? Sassy is searching for her parents! She doesn't want your damned money!"

"Women like her always want money. And

you keep out of this, Jett! You're the one who enabled this gold digger to brainwash my family. As of right now, you're fired."

"That suits me fine. Because as long as you're calling the shots for this ranch, Bart, you need to have a lawyer that's just as nasty as you are."

The check in her hand felt like a piece of smelly garbage, one that she couldn't shred to pieces fast enough to suit her.

"I'm not interested in your money, Mr. Calhoun." She threw the particles of worthless paper onto his desk. "And you don't scare me with your money or your threats. You're nothing more than a sad bitter old man."

Jett took her by the hand. "Let's get out of here," he muttered.

They started out of the study, only to have Bart fling a parting shot at their backs, "You two are going to be sorry about this."

Jett shut the door behind them, then quickly tugged her toward the staircase landing. "We have to find Orin. Bart has actually lost his moorings or he honestly does know your mother!"

"Oh, God, Jett, this is incredible. Is it possible—about my mother? And that money—

He must be crazy! Why would he be doing this now?"

"Let's not speculate." He touched her cheek and then cupped a protective hand to her little belly. "Are you okay?"

The tender concern in Jett's eyes was more than enough to wipe away Bart's insults.

"Yes, I'm fine." She laid her hand over his. "And Jett, later—when we're alone—I will listen."

He pressed a quick kiss on her cheek. "Yes. We'll talk it all out later, my darling. Right now, let's find Orin."

They hurried down the stairs and were crossing an expanse of hallway when they met Tessa carrying a tray loaded with an insulated coffee pot.

She paused to greet them. "Jett, Miss Matthews, how are you two doing this evening?"

"We're hunting Orin. Do you have any idea if he's in the house?"

"Surely. I'm taking his coffee to the family room right now. Follow me," she invited with a warm smile. "I'm sure he'll be glad to see you."

They followed the maid to the end of the hallway and into the same room where Sassy had first met the Calhoun family what now seemed like eons ago.

The moment he spotted Sassy and Jett, Orin rose from his chair and walked over to meet them in the middle of the room.

"Sassy. Jett. This is a really nice surprise." He kissed Sassy's cheek and gestured for them to take a seat on the couch. "Come sit and have coffee. Is there enough for the three of us in that pot, Tessa? If not, go have Greta make more. And please bring us some of those chocolate cookies. The ones with the gooey stuff inside."

"Yes, Mr. Calhoun. I'll be right back with those."

As the maid left the room, Jett said, "We'd like to sit and visit, Orin, but something has just happened. We think—" He looked at Sassy, then back to Orin. "Well, we just came from Bart's study. And he's saying some weird things."

Orin suddenly looked very worried. "You mean you think he's had a stroke? Was he slurring his words?"

"No. But if he was, it would've been because of the bourbon he was throwing back, not a stroke."

"Bourbon! My God!" Orin's confused gaze

vacillated between Jett and Sassy. "What were you two doing up there anyway? The way Bart feels about Sassy—"

"He called and demanded that we come," Jett explained.

"He tried to pay me off to leave," Sassy added. "I tore up the check and we left the room."

Jett said, "Orin, he implied that he knows Sassy's mother, but he wouldn't explain. I think we need to confront him about this."

The concerned look on Orin's face was suddenly replaced with outright anger. "Confront him? Hell, I'm going to choke the truth out of him!"

Orin left the room in long strides, leaving Jett and Sassy hurrying to keep up with him. When they reached the door of Bart's study, Orin didn't bother knocking—he burst through it.

Across the room, Bart was on his feet, pouring another measure of bourbon into his glass and he didn't bother glancing around until Orin yelled.

"Put it down, Dad! Now!"

As Orin went over to Bart's desk, Sassy was surprised to see the older man obey his son's command.

"What the hell are you two doing back here?" Bart shot at Jett and Sassy. "I told you both to beat it!"

Ignoring him, Jett led Sassy over to a nearby couch, and as she took a seat on an end cushion she realized just how much she needed to get off her feet. Her legs were shaking, and if Jett hadn't been sitting beside her, holding both her hands, they would have been shaking, too.

"Forget about them." Orin pointed to the scraps of torn check on the desktop. "I want to know what this is."

"That, my good son, is an attempt to save this family's reputation—to hold it together."

"Don't you mean an attempt to save yourself?" Orin countered. "Look, Dad, there's no use in this. Jett and I found the checks you wrote nearly twenty-five years ago. The DNA test will be back any day now. After that, you won't be able to hide."

Sassy was amazed to see a look of utter confusion come over the elder Calhoun.

"What are you talking about? You think I'm trying to protect myself?" Bart asked. Then, with a snort, he gestured to the whiskey. "You'd better drink that yourself. You're going to need it."

Orin glanced helplessly over his shoulder to Sassy and Jett before turning to confront his father again.

"Look, Dad, I don't want this to be a brawl between us. At its best, your blood pressure is high. None of us want you back in the hospital—or, God forbid, dead. But this farce of yours needs to come to an end. Whatever it is, we'll deal with it. You're human, you made a mistake. Let's get beyond it. You have eyes. You can see that Sassy is a carbon copy of Darci. That she looks enough like Finn to be his twin."

To everyone's surprise Bart chuckled with amazement, then pointed to the chair sitting at an angle to his desk. "You need to hear this sitting down, Orin."

"I'm fine where I am. Just spit it out. Or my sons and I are out of here—this ranch be damned!"

Jerking the glasses off his nose, Bart motioned to Sassy and Jett. "Come over here, you two. You need to hear this just as much as Orin."

With Jett's hand supporting her elbow, they walked over to join Orin in front of the desk, and as the three of them stood there facing the Calhoun patriarch, the whole thing suddenly felt surreal. Was she finally going to learn the identity of her real parents?

The question had her reaching for Jett's hand and clinging tightly to his fingers. Without this man at her side, nothing would be the same. Her zest for life would be gone. She had to believe he truly loved her. Had to believe it with all her heart or else her hopes and dreams would be gone.

Leaning back in the big leather desk chair, Bart studied the three of them. "Up until a few minutes ago, it never occurred to me that you all had assumed I had sired Sassy. Now that I think about it, I feel pretty flattered. 'Course, I would've only been about fifty-seven or -eight when she was conceived. I was still quite a hoss at that time. But I was crazy about my wife. Not one time did I ever cheat on her. Never even wanted to. Unlike someone else I know."

When his gaze landed accusingly on Orin, the man's eyes flew wide with shock.

"Why are you looking at me? I never—" He broke off, his head shaking with confusion. "Sassy can't be my daughter! I would've known if I'd had a daughter somewhere!"

Bart let out a weary sigh. "Sorry, Orin, but you need to do some hard remembering.

Back to when Darci died and Claudia was going around with a vacant stare. She barely acknowledged anyone around here, including you. I could see you were hurting and lonely. I just didn't realize how much until Marcia Stapleton contacted me."

Sassy watched the color drain from Orin's face as realization washed over him.

"You? Why did she contact you instead of me?" Orin asked in a low, strained voice.

Bart shrugged. "I'm not exactly sure why. The way she explained it, she said you two had a very brief affair and that you ended it and wouldn't have anything else to do with her. In a nutshell, I suppose she believed she could get more out of me. So I paid her the money she wanted, and she promised to keep in touch with me and let me know about the baby once it was born. But she didn't keep her part of the bargain."

Sassy was completely stunned. Orin was her father? Finn and his brothers were her brothers, too? It was incredible!

Unable to hold back any longer, she spoke up, "What were your intentions, Mr. Calhoun? Did you actually want to be involved with the baby? Or make sure she kept it away from the family?"

Now that the truth had come out, Bart actually looked ashamed and suddenly she had hope. Maybe there was a thread of conscience in this hard man, after all.

"Damn it, I'm not the heartless bastard everyone makes me out to be. As far as I was concerned, I would've taken you right in as soon as you were born. You were my son's own flesh and blood. His daughter, for God's sake. But I had to weigh the consequences. I had to consider Orin and his marriage. At that time Claudia was one step away from a breakdown. To learn that her husband had cheated on her and created a child with another woman—especially after she'd just lost her own child—well, I figured it would have been too much for her to bear. So I decided I would stay in contact with Marcia and make sure the child was well cared for until Claudia got emotionally stronger and I could have the baby brought here to the ranch."

"Why didn't that happen?" Jett demanded.

"That's what I'd like to know," Orin added in a dazed voice.

Bart picked up the whiskey glass and when he took a long sip Orin didn't try to stop him. "That's a piece of the puzzle that I can't figure out. Suddenly she stopped calling and I had no address to contact her. I couldn't find out if she'd carried the child full term or if she'd aborted it. Eventually I hired a P.I. to track her down, but that didn't work, either. And then, a few years ago, just by chance I saw her name listed in the obituaries of the *Reno Gazette.* She'd died at the age of forty-nine but there was no cause given. The short piece only listed the dates of her birth and death and that she'd been living in Espanola, New Mexico. From what I could gather, some acquaintance of hers there in Espanola had sent the bit of news to the paper because she'd known Marcia was originally from the area."

She'd heard her real mother's name and then, before she could catch her breath from that dizzying shock, Sassy learned the woman was dead. It was more than her brain could digest.

Orin rose from the chair and looked down at his father. "You should have told me all of this when Marcia first contacted you. It was wrong to keep it from me, Dad. And it was wrong to try and hide it now! Sassy is totally innocent in all of this and you've treated her like a dirty piece of garbage. That's the part I don't think I'll ever be able to forgive you for!"

"I didn't want all of this ugliness exposed.

That's why I've been trying to send Sassy on her way." Bart spluttered. "Look, Orin, I did this all for you. To save you from a divorce and disgrace. You're the one who sneaked past the boundaries of your marriage vows. And I sure as hell didn't raise you to behave that way! Maybe I did make a mess of this. But you're the one who initially caused it!"

Clearly torn apart by his father's revelation, Orin thrust a hand through his hair and began to pace around the room. But after one round, he came back to stand next to Sassy and, with a look of regretful agony, reached for her hand.

"I don't know what to say, Sassy. My association with Marcia was so very brief and insignificant that I put it out of my mind immediately after it happened. Even when Jett and I were trying to come up with clues to your parents, I wasn't thinking about myself. If Marcia had told me about this from the very beginning, things would've been different. And if Dad had told me, I would have done everything in my power to find you and bring you into my family. I hope you can believe that."

Squeezing Orin's hand, she gave him a wobbly smile. "I do believe you, Orin."

Jett wasn't so quick to let matters lie. He looked at Bart. "Okay, Bart. I'll give you credit for coming clean now. But why didn't you do this when Sassy first arrived instead of playing some sort of deceptive game with her and your own family? This happened so long ago, why go to such lengths to hide it now?"

Bart let out a heavy sigh. "Once a deception starts it's hard to stop it, Jett. I knew that Orin was going to be furious with me—that was something I could deal with. But I didn't want my grandsons to see their father in a skewed light. They all worship the ground he walks on. To learn that he cheated on their mother, a mother they loved so dearly—well, I didn't want that for them. I don't want it now."

Orin slanted him a dour glance. "The truth can't be helped, Dad. I don't want to lower myself in my son's eyes, but they deserve to be with their sister. And I pray to God that, in the process of getting to know her, they'll come to forgive me. And you!"

Unable to contain the emotions swelling her chest and throat, Sassy threw her arms around Orin, but her tears were coming so hard and fast it was impossible for her to tell him exactly what it meant to learn that he was her father.

"Oh, Sassy, you're my daughter. My own beautiful daughter." Over the top of her head, Orin looked gratefully over to Jett. "Thank you, Jett. Thank you for bringing my little girl to me."

Hours later, Jett and Sassy finally arrived back home, and by then she was so drained from the emotional upheaval she practically fell to the ground as Jett helped her out of the truck.

Not taking any chances, he immediately scooped her up into his arms and started to the front entrance of the house.

"Jett! I'm not going to faint," she protested, albeit feebly. "I can walk."

"Be quiet, Sassy, and let me take care of you."

Once inside, he carried her straight to her bedroom and gently sat her on the side of the bed. By then, Sassy was grateful for his help as he pulled off her coat and gently eased her back against a propped pillow.

With her head nestled on the soft down and her tired muscles giving way to the comfort of the mattress, she watched as he removed the suitcases and clothes she'd left at the foot of the bed when they'd rushed off to the Silver Horn.

After he piled the lot into a nearby chair, he asked, "Where are you nightclothes?"

She pointed to the chest of drawers. "In the top drawer. But I'll get them later. I'm not an invalid."

Ignoring her, he rifled through the drawers until he found her pajamas and robe. "I'm angry at myself for not bringing you home sooner. But for a while there things were so chaotic. The guys were all so excited to learn they had a sister, I couldn't just drag you away without giving them some time with you."

A weary smile curved the corners of Sassy's lips. "It's all like a dream, Jett. I have brothers! And they treated me like I was their real sister."

"You are one of them, Sassy." Carrying the bedclothes over to her, he eased onto the edge of the mattress. "Let me help you change, and then I'll go get you something nice and warm to drink."

"I thought we were going to talk," she said as she began to unbutton her blouse.

"We are. After I'm sure you're comfortable and resting."

He helped her into her pajamas, and after she'd settled back against the pillows once again, he left the bedroom to go fetch the drink.

While he was gone, Sassy closed her eyes and willed her whirling thoughts to slow enough to enable her to digest all the incredible things that had happened since she and Jett had raced over to the Silver Horn earlier this evening.

She was a Calhoun! Even now that the initial shock was over, the idea still hadn't completely sunk in for her. She'd gone from having no parents to having her own living, breathing father. She'd never had siblings and now she had five wonderful brothers. And when her baby was born it was going to have uncles and a second grandfather. Her baby was going to have the family roots it needed and deserved. The wonderful realization was still too much for her to comprehend in one short evening.

But learning she was a part of the Calhoun family and figuring out her place in it was not the thing that was dominating her thoughts right now. Her happiness, her whole future depended on Jett. She wanted her home to be more than this house. She wanted it to be in his heart.

Her thoughts were suddenly interrupted as the door opened and Jett entered carrying a large mug. As she watched him come to her, a sweet, hungry longing filled her, and she realized that her journey to Nevada had given her more than she could have imagined. Not only had she found her family, she'd learned what love was really all about. The question now was whether Jett had learned it or had merely been mouthing words he knew she wanted to hear.

Sitting beside her, he carefully handed the mug to her. "I made you some hot chocolate. Maybe it will help revive you."

"Thanks. I'm already feeling better." Wrapping both hands around the warm mug, she took two long sips before asking, "Is Bella already in bed? I didn't see her when we came in a few minutes ago."

"I ran into her in the kitchen, and while I made the hot chocolate I explained everything that happened at the Horn."

"Was she as shocked as I still am?" Sassy asked.

Jett chuckled. "Bella works in a law office. Nothing surprises her anymore." He stroked a hand along the calf of her leg. "She's very happy that you've found your family. And so am I."

With his head slightly bent, the light from the lamp glistened over the waves of his dark hair. Sassy itched to set the mug aside and reach for him, to slide her hands through his rumpled hair and drag his mouth down to hers. So many days had passed since she'd been in his arms and she'd spent each one of those days aching to be near him, yet determined to keep her distance. Now, just the brief memory of his saying how much she meant to him was chipping away at her resistance.

"Are you?"

He looked up to meet her gaze. "I don't know where that question is coming from. From the very start I've wanted you to find the identity of your real parents. I'm just sorry that your mother is gone and you'll never be able to know her."

She sighed. "I'm not sure that she and I would've ever had much of a relationship, Jett. The past probably would've always stood between us. But I'm going to try not to judge her. Especially when I'll never know what was going on in her life—the troubles she might have been going through. For all we know she could've been frightened and running from someone, and left me at the orphanage in order to make sure I was safe."

"You're right. We don't know her circumstances. So I hope you can forgive her. After all, she did carry you for nine months and give birth to you. That has to count for a lot."

She nodded. "I have forgiven her already, Jett."

Leaning closer, he asked, "What about me? Have you decided to forgive me?"

Her heart began to thump at a high rate. "You said some unforgivable things to me and Noah. You even fired him. That was—"

"Noah isn't fired," he corrected her. "I apologized to him as soon as you two returned to the barn. And fortunately he understood and forgave me for behaving like a jealous idiot. The question now is, do you pardon me for not recognizing days ago how much I love you?"

Doubt and hope tussled inside her as she searched the depths of his brown eyes. This man had stood by her side from the very beginning. She had to believe he would remain there for the rest of their lives.

"Love? Days ago?" she questioned.

Groaning, he plucked the mug from her hands and placed it on the nightstand before he gathered her into the circle of his arms. "Oh, my darling Sassy, when I saw you getting ready to leave it was like someone had stabbed me with a knife. I love you. I can't let you go. You and the baby mean more to me than anything. I want us to be married. I want the three of us to be a family. A real family with love tying us all together."

She eased her head back from his shoulder to look at him. "But your marriage to Erica was—"

He cut her off. "Was wrong from the start, Sassy. I didn't understand what she was going through or why she was behaving so irrationally. All the time I was trying to give her what she needed, I didn't understand she simply wanted my heart." With both hands, he gently cradled her face. "I feel guilty about that now, Sassy. But I also feel so very, very blessed that you've come along and taught me that love is real and powerful and means more than anything I can buy or touch or see."

Tears of joy rushed to her eyes. "Oh, Jett, do you really mean that?"

"If you'll let me, I'm going to spend the rest

of my life showing you exactly how much I mean it. Do I get the chance?"

Her soft laugh fanned his face. "Now that I've caught my cowboy, I'm not about to let him go."

Bending his head, he placed a long, tender kiss on her lips.

"Does that mean you're going to let me lie down beside you?"

Enchanted by the masculine beauty of his face, she traced a finger along the bottom of his lip. "What is Bella going to think if you don't come out of my bedroom tonight?"

A clever grin twisted his lips. "She's going to think her brother has finally come to his senses."

Laughing softly, Sassy scooted across the mattress to make room for him, and once she was tucked into the curve of his body, her cheek resting against his shoulder, she realized her search had ended. She was finally home to stay.

Epilogue

Ten months later, a soft autumn sky shed a hazy light across the open range, coating the purple sage and creosote bushes with a golden hue. As the old work truck bumped over the cattle trail, Sassy clung tightly to the baby in her arms while her husband kept darting surreptitious glances at the two of them.

A few short days after she'd learned she was a Calhoun, their small but beautiful wedding had taken place on the Silver Horn. Like a proud father, Orin had given her away, while Bella had acted as her maid of honor. Somehow Jett had talked Noah into standing as his best man, and a thrilled Finn had been a proud groomsman. In spite of the short notice, Frankie Cantrell and her daughter, Alexa, had flown to Nevada to attend the ceremony and meet Sassy's new family. Her brothers had told her it was the first time they'd had a party in the house since their mother had died and everyone had enjoyed the celebration.

Six months after the wedding, shortly after the Fourth of July, Joshua Jett Sundell, J.J. for short, had been born. "A little live fire-cracker" Jett often called their son, and given his bright red hair and temperament to match, Sassy agreed that the moniker was fitting. Right after J.J.'s birth she'd contacted Barry's father in Colorado to tell him about the baby. Douglas Landers had been very grateful to hear that a part of his son lived on and had come to see the baby a few weeks later. Jett and Sassy had taken an immediate liking to the man and had invited him to come as often as he wished to visit his grandchild.

As for the Calhoun family, since the night Bart had revealed the truth about her parentage, many changes had taken place. Bart was learning he couldn't earn forgiveness from anyone by making demands or threats. Amazingly he was beginning to soften somewhat and seemed to be trying to loosen the tight rein he'd tried to keep over everyone on the Silver Horn. As for Orin, Sassy was growing closer and closer to her father. The more time she spent with him, the more she understood that his brief connection to Marcia Stapleton had never been planned. With Claudia shutting him out, he'd been in a lonely and vulnerable state and Marcia had recognized him as easy and wealthy prey. And from her brothers' reactions to learning about their father's indiscretions, she could see they also understood how it had happened. The only question left was why Marcia had cut all ties to Bart, but the fact that she was dead and gone made that part of the puzzle seem insignificant now.

Pulling her thoughts back to the present, Sassy asked, "Exactly where are you taking us, Jett? It's almost supper time and Bella is cooking pork chops. They'll be cold before we can get back."

"Don't worry," he assured her. "This trip will be worth eating a cold chop. I promise."

With a good-natured roll of her eyes, she kissed her son's cheek. "J.J., I think your daddy has something on his mind that he's not telling us."

Jett chuckled. "Actually, I do have something on my mind. I've been thinking about the ranch and how well it's been doing. Cattle prices are up and it's time we started expanding and adding to the herd. I was talking to our neighbor, Jim Flores, the other day and he hinted that he might be willing to sell some of the land that adjoins us."

"That sounds exciting. When do we start?"

Smiling smugly, he said, "Oh, how about as soon as we top this next rise?"

Sassy was trying to figure out what he meant by that, when the trail took them over a low hill and there, spread across the range in front of them, was a huge herd of Black Angus cattle nipping at the dried autumn grass.

Her mouth flopped open as he braked the truck to a halt. "Where did those come from? I didn't know you bought more cattle! There must be fifty or sixty head out there!"

"Exactly one hundred. Orin thought that would be a nice round number."

"Orin? What's he got to do with this?"

She shifted in the seat so that she was facing him and he automatically reached to take J.J. from her. As he settled the baby in the crook of his arm, he said, "Those cattle are a gift to his first and only grandson and to you."

Slapping a hand over her gaping mouth, she stared out the window. The herd represented a small fortune.

"Oh, Jett, this is too much." Ever since Bart had revealed the truth about her parentage, Sassy had refused to take anything from the Calhouns. She'd even had Jett write up a document stating she wouldn't receive money or gifts from the family, but Orin had torn up the paper, just as she'd torn up Bart's check. It was all about what was behind the giving, she realized. And accepting Orin's gesture of love was far more important than proving she wasn't a gold digger.

"According to Orin it's not nearly enough. So I wouldn't be surprised if he didn't show up with more gifts in the coming months. He can see his daughter is becoming a fine ranch woman and that makes him very proud. It makes me very proud, too," he added.

Reaching over, she squeezed his knee. "All those years I worked as a maid I used to dream about what I'd like to be if I ever got the chance to go to college. But I could never think of one thing that I could really connect to. I thought I lacked ambition or something. 'Cause what I always enjoyed the most was going down to the barns and spending time with the cows and horses. Maybe that wasn't a bad thing after all." She shot her husband an impish grin. "Now that I'm married to a rancher."

He grunted with amusement. "If I remember right, you once called me a lawyer disguised as a cowboy. I guess I'm a bit of both."

"You're a very fine lawyer, too," she said with obvious pride. "That's why you're getting more clients every day."

"Well, I never expected to build a clientele overnight. And since I only work in town three days a week, that makes building my private law practice a slow process. But the clients are beginning to come."

Her expression turned serious. "Are you sorry you agreed to stay and work as the Calhouns' lawyer the other two days of the week? I know how much Orin and my brothers wanted you to still be a part of the Silver Horn. And, to be honest, so did I."

"I'm not sorry about anything, Sassy. With you as my wife I feel like I'm part of the Calhoun family, too. When Orin begged me to stay on, I couldn't refuse him. And with Bella helping me with the Silver Horn projects, the workload there is much lighter now. But branching out with my own law office has given me a new sense of purpose in my legal work." He reached across the seat and patted her cheek. "Let's get out and take a closer look at the cattle. We can always put those chops in the microwave."

Laughing, she agreed, and they left the confines of the truck to walk closer to the grazing cattle.

Standing close to Sassy's side, and with their son snuggled against his chest, Jett pointed toward the herd.

"Look at the cows, J.J.," he said to the boy. "By the time their babies have babies you might have a little brother or sister. What do you think about that?"

J.J. was looking around him with wonder and Sassy knew that years from now, when he was old enough to appreciate the story, his parents would tell him about the day he first became a real cattleman.

"I don't know what J.J. thinks about that idea," Sassy said with a naughty grin, "but I think we need to go home and talk about this in the bedroom. Between the sheets."

"And in my arms," Jett added.

He leaned over and pressed a kiss to her lips. When he lifted his head, Sassy sighed with contentment. "You know, we're making this ranch into a mighty fine place."

His smile full of love, he touched a fingertip to the end of her nose. "A mighty fine ranch. And the home I always wanted. Our home."

An overflow of emotions suddenly glazed her eyes with tears. "Oh, Jett—"

"Aw, honey, what's wrong?"

She smiled through her tears. "I'm just thinking back to when I first came here to Nevada. I was pregnant and so alone. Now I have you and our son. And I'm so happy."

With the baby's cheek resting against his, he used his free arm to curl around her shoulders and draw her close to his side. "Before you came, my darling wife, I thought I had all I needed. But you showed me that a man doesn't have anything until he has love."

* * * * *

Visit
ReaderService.com
Today!

**As a valued member of the
Harlequin Reader Service,
you'll find these benefits and more at
ReaderService.com:**

- Try 2 free books from any series
- Access risk-free special offers
- View your account history & manage payments
- Browse the latest Bonus Bucks catalog

Don't miss out!

If you want to stay up-to-date on the latest at the Harlequin Reader Service and enjoy more content, make sure you've signed up for our monthly News & Notes email newsletter. Sign up online at ReaderService.com or by calling Customer Service at 1-800-873-8635.

RS20